"Your wife may now reveal her face."

Sheikh Sharif Bin Noor Al Nazar waited with bated breath as his new wife's attendants came forward to unhook the elaborate mask that had hidden her face for the duration of the wedding ceremony.

Not even her eyes had been visible.

Sharif couldn't care less what she looked like—he had no intention of consummating this marriage. It was to be in name only for as short amount of time as possible—but if she was at least passably attractive, that would certainly make things easier for him.

The delicate chains and gold medallions of the covering clinked as it was removed and her face was revealed.

The first thing Sharif noted somewhat dispassionately was that he didn't have to worry about her being passably attractive—because she was stunningly beautiful.

The second was more of a visceral reaction. Shock, followed quickly by anger. Because Aaliyah was far from being the stranger he'd expected—was not in fact a stranger.

Not at all. In fact he knew her intimately.

One word resounded in Sharif's head. He wasn't even sure if he uttered it out loud. *"You!"*

The Marchetti Dynasty

They live a superrich lifestyle—but for this dynasty to survive, these brothers need brides!

The Marchetti name is synonymous with luxury— their family business boasts the most opulent brands from fashion to real estate. While the three Marchetti brothers live a superrich existence and have no trouble attracting women, they know little about love and have even less in common, apart from the emotional scars of their dysfunctional relationships with their unscrupulous father—and their resulting bachelor statuses! Now they are going to have to work together to protect their inheritance—and securing the Marchetti dynasty will mean learning that gaining wives and heirs is going to take far more than a little seduction!

Meet the Marchetti brothers and the feisty and resourceful women who tame them in:

Nikos and Maggie's story:
The Maid's Best Kept Secret

Maks and Zoe's story:
The Innocent Behind the Scandal

Sharif and Aaliyah's story:
Bride Behind the Desert Veil

All available now!

Abby Green

—

BRIDE BEHIND THE
DESERT VEIL

Recycling programs
for this product may
not exist in your area.

ISBN-13: 978-1-335-40402-2

Bride Behind the Desert Veil

Copyright © 2021 by Abby Green

All rights reserved. No part of this book may be used or reproduced in
any manner whatsoever without written permission except in the case of
brief quotations embodied in critical articles and reviews.

This is a work of fiction. Names, characters, places and incidents
are either the product of the author's imagination or are used fictitiously.
Any resemblance to actual persons, living or dead, businesses,
companies, events or locales is entirely coincidental.

This edition published by arrangement with Harlequin Books S.A.

For questions and comments about the quality of this book,
please contact us at CustomerService@Harlequin.com.

Harlequin Enterprises ULC
22 Adelaide St. West, 40th Floor
Toronto, Ontario M5H 4E3, Canada
www.Harlequin.com

Printed in U.S.A.

Irish author **Abby Green** ended a very glamorous career in film and TV—which really consisted of a lot of standing in the rain outside actors' trailers—to pursue her love of romance. After she'd bombarded Harlequin with manuscripts, they kindly accepted one, and an author was born. She lives in Dublin, Ireland, and loves any excuse for distraction. Visit abby-green.com or email abbygreenauthor@gmail.com.

Books by Abby Green

Harlequin Presents

Awakened by the Scarred Italian
The Greek's Unknown Bride

One Night With Consequences

An Innocent, A Seduction, A Secret

The Marchetti Dynasty

The Maid's Best Kept Secret
The Innocent Behind the Scandal

Rival Spanish Brothers

Confessions of a Pregnant Cinderella
Redeemed by His Stolen Bride

Visit the Author Profile page
at Harlequin.com for more titles.

This is for Ellen Walsh. We've been best friends since we were skinny little nippers running around the back fields and cliff ways of Ballybunion. I treasure our friendship and the roots from which it came. Love you lots, always.

PROLOGUE

'YOUR WIFE MAY now reveal her face.'

Sheikh Sharif Bin Noor Al Nazar waited with bated breath as his new wife's attendants came forward to unhook the elaborate face mask that had covered her face for the duration of the wedding ceremony.

Not even her eyes had been visible.

Sharif couldn't care less what she looked like—he had no intention of consummating this marriage; it was to be in name only for as short amount of time as possible—but if she was at least passably attractive that would certainly make things easier for him.

The delicate chains and gold medallions of the face covering clinked as it was removed and her face was revealed.

The first thing Sharif noted somewhat dispassionately was that he didn't have to worry about her being passably attractive—because she was stunningly beautiful.

The second thing was more of a visceral reaction. Shock, followed quickly by anger. Because his new wife, far from being the stranger he'd expected, was not in fact a stranger.

Not at all. In fact he knew her intimately.

One word resounded in Sharif's head. He wasn't even sure if he uttered it out loud. *'You!'*

CHAPTER ONE

Two weeks ago

'YOU'RE SAYING YOU don't even know what your bride-to-be looks like?'

The horrified expression on Nikos Marchetti's face was almost comical. Sharif Marchetti's younger half-brother was on a video call from his home in Ireland, where Sharif could see his wife, Maggie, pregnant again, pottering in the background with their eight-month-old baby son, Daniel, on one arm. For some strange reason Sharif found the domestic scene presented before him...distracting.

Because it was catching at something inside him. A place it shouldn't be catching. Because he found such domesticity utterly alien and unwelcome.

He focused on his brother. 'No, I don't know what she looks like. I know nothing about her and I'm not interested. I'm marrying her because of a diplomatic agreement between Al-Murja and Taraq that has to be honoured. And,' he tacked on with studied nonchalance, 'because settling down appears to be good for business.'

That was an understatement. Since both his younger

half-brothers had recently taken wives—Maks, their youngest brother, had married his wife in a private civil ceremony in London just before Christmas—the Marchetti Group's stock value had gone through the roof.

But Sharif knew it could go even higher, reaching a stability and value that would finally bring him close to achieving all he'd set out to achieve when his father had died. When the old man had finally relinquished his control over the company that had been built off the backs of the fortunes of others. Namely, each one of his three wives—Sharif's mother, and the mothers of Nikos and Maks.

Maggie's face, and Daniel's cherubic one, appeared over Nikos's shoulder. 'Al-Murja and Taraq? An arranged marriage? It all sounds so exotic!'

Sharif wrangled his focus back to the present moment. Nikos was reaching for his son, tucking him competently against his chest while commenting drily to his wife, who had come to perch on his knee, 'Sharif doesn't operate at the level of mere mortals. On this side of the world he's a Marchetti, and merely one of the world's most successsful billionaires, but in his mother's desert home of Al-Murja he's a royal sheikh and even goes by a different name.'

Maggie's big blue eyes opened wide. 'Ooh, Sharif, I never knew that. What's your other name?'

There was a knock on the door of Sharif's office in Manhattan. He welcomed it, not liking how this familiarity was impacting upon him. Over the last few months he and his brothers might have developed more of an affinity than they'd ever had before, but they were still far from being truly functional as a family.

'My car is here. I'll be in touch, Nikos, as soon as I'm back.'

His brother shook his head. 'Why are you doing this again?'

Sharif forced a smile he wasn't feeling. 'Because I'm envious of what you and Maks have, brother. I want to be as happy as you.'

But as Sharif terminated the connection on Nikos's sharp burst of disbelieving laughter, his deep-seated cynicism rubbed against something raw. Something he knew would only be made less raw when he stood over the dismantled pieces of the Marchetti Group and ground his father's legacy to dust.

His conscience pricked as he sat in the back of his chauffeur-driven limousine a few minutes later, thinking of his half-brothers and how they might react if they knew his plans. But he quashed the feeling. They had no more allegiance to their father than he had. And, as much as they might have developed an affinity, he didn't trust anyone with his plans. Not even them.

When the time came he would tell them and they would walk away with wealth beyond their means.

What more could they want?

One week ago, Taraq

'Why should I let you take your sister's place for this marriage?' asked the King.

Aaliyah Binte Rashad Mansour did her best to stay calm, but she was gritty-eyed from lack of sleep after the frantic journey she'd just taken from England back to her desert home in the middle of the Arabian Peninsula, after an hysterical phone call from her beloved younger half-sister Samara.

'Because I'm your eldest daughter. Samara is only nineteen.'

And she was in love with the son of the King's chief aide.

Liyah's father said nothing more for a moment, and she pressed on while she had a chance. 'Samara hasn't even met this man you want her to marry. Clearly they're strangers. What does it matter if it's me and not her?'

Her sister had told her, *'He just wants a wife. He doesn't care who that is, as long as it's someone from this family.'*

Her father made an indistinct sound. He wasn't a very tall man. Liyah was almost taller, at five foot ten. She'd always felt that he disapproved of her less than delicate proportions. Among the myriad other things that she'd never understood.

Her mother had been his first wife, and she had died when Liyah was a toddler. Liyah had only the vaguest memories of being rocked, and a lullaby being sung, but she'd long since convinced herself that was just a weak fantasy to make up for the fact that when her father had married again and had his other children, Liyah had been effectively sidelined and forgotten about. Neglected.

The only family member Liyah had ever allowed close was Samara who, since she was tiny, had followed Liyah around like a faithful shadow, crashing through all of Liyah's barriers.

As soon as she'd known Samara was in distress, and

why, Liyah hadn't thought twice about coming home and offering herself in her sister's place. But now that she was here in front of her father a sense of panic gripped her.

'Who is he, anyway? And why is he happy to marry a woman he doesn't even know? I thought we'd moved on from arranged marriages.'

'Don't be naive, Aaliyah. The best marriages are still primarily the ones that are arranged for the benefit of two parties—in this instance two neighbouring kingdoms that have a long history of enmity.'

'But it's been years since anything—'

Her father interrupted. 'He's the cousin of the King of Al-Murja and he's honouring a decades-old diplomatic agreement by marrying into this family and providing a dowry. His mother was meant to marry your uncle, but she took off to Europe and married an Italian playboy instead, giving him her dowry. That marriage fell apart and she came home in disgrace with a baby son. She died when he was still young and his father brought him up.'

That story rang a few vague bells in Liyah's head. But her father had stopped pacing and now looked at her. There was a gleam in his dark eyes—very unlike Liyah's green ones.

'His mother ran off to Europe just as you did. Clearly you share her rebellious spirit, Aaliyah.'

Indignation made Liyah's spine tense. 'It's hardly rebellious to want to—'

Her father held up a hand, cutting her off again. 'No, I think this will work very well, actually. Sheikh Sharif Bin Noor Al Nazar controls a vast luxury conglomerate in Europe. He will not stand for a rebellious wife. He is just what you need to learn some control, Aaliyah. To learn respect.'

A million things bubbled in Liyah's blood, chief of which were a very familiar hurt and the need to defend herself, but she forced herself to swallow it all down and ask, 'So does this mean that you'll let me take Samara's place?'

Her father looked at her for a long moment. There wasn't a hint of warmth or approval in his eyes. Just the cool disdain that had become so familiar. Then he said, 'Yes, you will be the one to marry Sheikh Sharif Bin Noor Al Nazar. And you will use this as an opportunity to redeem yourself in the eyes of this family.'

Liyah's relief was tempered with panic at what she'd just done, but she couldn't back out now. Not when Samara's happiness was at stake. She would do anything for her sister.

Her father was turning away from her, clearly done with the conversation, and shock that he could dismiss her so easily after all but handing her over to a complete stranger for the rest of her life made Liyah blurt out, 'Why do you care for me so little, Father?'

He stopped. He faced her again, and for the first time in her life Liyah saw something flicker to life in his eyes. Incredibly. It was only after he spoke that she realised what it was: acute pain.

He said, 'Because your mother was the only woman I loved and you look exactly like her. So every day that you're alive and she isn't is a reminder of what I have lost.'

Yesterday

Sharif saw the falcon first. A peregrine falcon. Mature. He guessed at least ten years old. Magnificent. Feathers reflecting golden tints in the dying rays of the sun. Its grace and seemingly lazy circles in the air didn't fool Sharif. It was looking for prey and would swoop and kill within a split second.

He was about to find his binoculars to have a closer look when he heard the sound of a horse's hooves. One horse.

He shrank back into the shadows of the trees around the natural pool at the oasis where he'd set up camp for the night, en route to the palace at Taraq. His team had gone on ahead. He needed some time alone in the desert. It never failed to ground and recharge him, and he knew the coming weeks would require all of his focus…

A horse and rider thundered into the small but lush oasis, shattering the peace. In an instant Sharif assessed the young man to be an expert horseman, his body moving as one with the horse. The enormous stallion came to an abrupt halt under a twitch of the reins, nostrils flaring, body sheened with a light film of sweat. He'd been ridden hard.

The young man slid off athletically, patting the horse's neck and leading it over to the pool where it drank thirstily. He looped the reins around a nearby tree, tethering the horse.

Sharif wasn't sure why he stayed hidden in the shadows, but some instinct was compelling him to remain hidden for now. He sensed the stranger's desire to be alone. Like him. Also, he presumed the rider would move on once the horse had drunk and rested for a moment.

He couldn't make out the man's—the *boy's* face. He had to be a boy. He was tall, but too slight to be a man. His head and face were covered in a loose turban.

The falcon swooped low at that moment and Sharif saw the rider lift up his right arm. The bird came to rest on a leather arm-guard. So it was a pet falcon. Impressive.

The stranger fed the bird what looked like a piece of meat out of a pouch at his hip and then, with a flick of his arm, let the bird fly off again.

The young man stood at the edge of the pool. A sigh seemed to go through his slender frame. And then he lifted his hands to undo his turban.

Sharif moved to announce himself, but stopped in his tracks when the turban fell away and a riotous mass of dark unruly curls was unleashed, tumbling down a narrow back. *Narrow back. Long hair. Curls.*

It hit Sharif. This wasn't a young man—it was a young woman, and as he watched, struck mute and unable to move, she started to take off all her clothes.

The gallop to the oasis had only taken the smallest edge off Liyah's turmoil—a potent mixture of anger and helplessness. It was the eve of her wedding and she was hopelessly trapped. And she'd put herself in this position for the sake of her sister, which only made her feel even more impotent. It wasn't as if she was being forced into this. She could have ignored her sister's call. Stayed in Europe.

Yet, she couldn't have. She adored her sister—the

only family member who had ever shown Liyah love and acceptance. Liyah would do anything to secure Samara's happiness. Even this.

And, after extracting a promise from her father that he wouldn't stand in the way of Samara marrying her sweetheart, Javid, at least Liyah's sacrifice wouldn't be in vain.

But it wasn't even that sacrifice that was uppermost in her mind. She was still reeling from what her father had revealed a week ago. That he'd loved her mother. And that Liyah reminded him of her.

Knowing the reason why she'd always been shunned by her father wasn't exactly a comfort. It only compounded her sense of dislocation. Isolation. Love had done this to her father—made him bitter.

In a way, discovering this had only confirmed her belief that love was not to be trusted. It made you weak and vulnerable.

If anything, she more than most should agree with a marriage based on the sound principles of practicality and necessity. She just hadn't ever figured that she would have to put it into practice. She'd relished the prospect of an independent life. Free to make choices of her own.

Living in Europe for the past couple of years had given her a false sense of freedom. That freedom had been an illusion. Even if she hadn't come back here to take her sister's place, her family's neglect and disapproval would have always cast a long shadow, reminding her of how unlovable she was.

Since her father had mentioned that her husband-to-be was the CEO of a luxury conglomerate, Liyah imagined him to be the sort of individual who gorged himself on rich food, beautiful women and vacuous pleasures.

She didn't want to blight her last days of freedom—*ha!*—by thinking of a future she couldn't change, so she hadn't even bothered to look him up. Which she knew wasn't exactly rational—but then she hadn't been feeling very rational for the last week as the full enormity of what she'd agreed to sank in.

The water of the deep pool looked inviting and cool and she felt hot and constricted. Panicky.

She let the turban that had been wound around her head and face to protect her from the sand drop to the ground. She started to take off her clothes, knowing she was safely alone because no one ever came here. It was too close to the palace to be a stopping point for travellers. And the Sheikh—her future husband—had arrived just before she'd left, with an entourage. Not that she'd hung around to see him.

She undid the buttons on her shirt and it fell down her arms with a soft whoosh. The cooling evening air made her skin prickle. She undid her bra, let that fall too. She opened the button on her soft leather trousers—trousers that her father would never approve of as they were not feminine. Which was precisely why Liyah loved them. Apart from the ease of movement they gave her.

She shimmied them over her hips and then down her legs, stepping out of them. She pulled down her underwear.

Now she was naked.

Her horse whinnied softly. The sky was a dark bruised lavender, filling with stars. A crescent moon was rising. A swell of emotion made her chest tight.

Would she ever be back here again? She loved this place. It was where she felt most at peace. Cantering over the sand with her bird high in the sky above her. Wild. Free.

Liyah stepped into the water, still warm after the day's intense heat. It glided over her skin like silk as she walked in up to her waist and then dived deep, where the depths were cooler and darker.

Only when her lungs were about to burst did she kick her way back up and break the surface, sucking in deep gulps of air. It took a second for her ears to clear before she heard a man's voice.

'What the hell were you doing? I was about to rescue you.'

At the sound of the voice Liyah whirled around in the water to face the shore. Shock at the sight of the very tall, broad and dark stranger almost made her sink under the surface again.

His hands were on his hips and he stood in the shallows, the end of his long white robe drifting in the water. He had short, thick dark hair. His jaw was stubbled. But even through her shock Liyah could see that he was breathtakingly handsome. And powerful.

His eyes looked dark too. High cheekbones. A firm mouth. Currently in a disapproving line.

That line of disapproval snapped Liyah out of her shock. She'd had enough disapproval to last a lifetime. Her peace had been invaded. Her last night of solitude.

'I don't need rescuing.' A thought occurred to her and an acute sense of exposure made her ask, 'How long have you been there?'

'Long enough.' He sounded grim. 'You need to come out.'

Indignation filled her at his autocratic tone, reminding her of how little autonomy she had over her own
life. 'I don't *need* to do anything, actually.'

'You're going to stay there all night? You'll freeze.'

It was true. The scorching desert temperatures fell
precipitously at night. Liyah could already feel the chill
of the water creeping into her bones.

'I can't come out. I don't have any clothes on.'
Strangely, she didn't feel unsafe, even though this man
was a complete stranger.

'I know.'

Liyah stopped treading water. 'You did spy on me.'

Yet, strangely again, the thought of him watching
her strip and dive into the water wasn't making her feel
indignant. It was making her feel…aware.

In the dusky half-light Liyah couldn't be entirely sure
she wasn't dreaming. She could have sworn there had
been no one else here when she'd arrived, but then, she
hadn't exactly checked her surroundings thoroughly.

When she looked over the man's shoulder now, she
could make out the shape of a tent amongst the trees on
the far side of the oasis. And a horse. It whinnied softly
and her horse answered.

'You're camping here?'

'For the night, yes.'

His voice was deep. Deep enough to reverberate in
the pit of her belly. He had an accent she couldn't place.
Mid-Atlantic, but with a hint of something else—something foreign. But also familiar to here. An intriguing
mix. Yet she knew she'd never seen him before. He was
a total stranger.

She should ask who he was, but for some reason the words wouldn't form on her tongue.

And he was right: she couldn't stay treading water all night.

'I need something to wear.' Her own clothes were scattered along the shoreline, but instead of going to pick them up the man reached behind his head and pulled off his robe.

Liyah's breath caught in her solar plexus when his bare chest was revealed. Massive and tightly muscled, with dark hair curling over his pectorals and a dark line dissecting his abdominals to disappear under the loosely fitting trousers that hung low on his lean hips.

'Here, take this.'

He held his robe outstretched to her from the shore. She swam towards the shallows until she could feel the ground beneath her feet. The water lapped around her shoulders.

She could see that the bottoms of his trousers were in the water. 'Your trousers are getting wet.'

'They'll dry.'

Again, Liyah wondered if she was in a dream. But no dream she'd ever had came close to this. She started to walk forward, feeling the resistance of the water against her body.

The waterline dropped lower, now just covering her breasts. Liyah stopped. She expected the man to turn around, to show some respect. But he didn't. *He'd already watched her.* Albeit from behind.

Again, it didn't make her feel violated in any way— it excited her.

If she was being rational for a second, *excited* was

the last thing she should be feeling. Scared. Wary. Insulted. Indignant. Those were the things she should be feeling. Yet she wasn't.

She should also be asking him to turn around. But, again, the words wouldn't form in her mouth. She was filled with a fire that made her feel rebellious and reckless. Surely just a reaction to everything that was happening to her—everything that was expected of her? But she had a sense that she was somehow regaining some control over a life that had veered wildly out of control.

She also had an overwhelming compulsion to go towards this complete stranger as she was. Naked.

She took another step forward. The water broke just over her breasts. Another step. Now her breasts were bared to the man's dark gaze. She could see him more clearly now. His eyes were dark. His jaw defined. Tight. His gaze dropped. Her nipples were already tight and hard from the water. They tingled.

She kept moving forward and the water lapped at her belly, then her hips, the tops of her legs and thighs. Between her legs, where the centre of her body pulsed with heat.

In some corner of her brain she was aghast at herself for behaving with such wanton confidence. She wasn't this person who would allow a stranger to see her naked body. But here, in this place—this place that had been a sacred refuge to her for her whole life—she felt removed from reality. Removed from the confines of normal behaviour.

And this man was more than just a random stranger. She'd sensed it the minute she'd laid eyes on him. He held himself with the arrogance and confidence of a born leader. Entitled. Proud.

She stepped into the shallows and reached for the robe he held out. She pulled it on over her head, aware of that dark gaze watching as the fine material settled over her body, the bottom wet from the water.

The heat from his body lingered on the robe and made her skin prickle even more. Her breasts felt heavy. Tight.

'Thank you.' She sounded breathless.

'You're welcome.'

Strangely, even though she was covered again from neck to toe, she didn't feel any more protected from that penetrating gaze. Up close, she realised he was even more magnificent. A virile man in his prime. Tall. Broad. With dark olive skin that gleamed under the rising moon, stretched taut over hard muscles.

He held out a hand and Liyah looked at it for a long moment. The air was heavy around her. Heavy with a tension that had nothing to do with conflict or conversation. It was a tension that came from the crackling energy between them. A tension that came from this whole improbable situation.

In all her years of coming here she'd never met anyone else. Ever. But tonight, on the eve of her wedding to a man sight unseen, here was this compelling stranger. She wasn't usually prone to superstition, but it felt somehow…fated.

Tomorrow her life would change for ever, but tomorrow wasn't here yet… There was a whole night between now and then. A whole night of tantalising freedom left. The last piece of freedom she would have for some time.

Before she could think about it she put her hand into his. It was big. Slightly callused. Something about that evidence of hard work thrilled her. His fingers closed around hers and he tugged her out of the shallows and onto the sand.

Sharif had wondered if he was hallucinating. If he'd conjured up the goddess who had disappeared into the black depths of the oasis pool. But then she'd emerged, like Aphrodite, dark olive skin glistening like satin as the water sluiced over her body.

She was no marble statue, cold and rigid and pale. She was all woman. Flesh and bone. Limbs long and sleek.

And the hand in his now felt real enough.

Instinctively his thumb felt for her pulse and it throbbed at her wrist, echoing the throb in his blood.

'You are real…' he said, almost to himself.

Even though she was covered again, her naked image was imprinted on his brain. For ever, he suspected. He had watched her disrobe, too transfixed to say a word. Her body was carved from an erotic fantasy he hadn't even realised he'd had—strong and supple, athletic, but with curves that pronounced her a fertile woman in her prime.

Wide hips, small waist, long legs, lush bottom. And her breasts… Bigger than he would have guessed. Firm. Perfectly formed, with dark nipples that made his mouth water.

Dark tight curls at the juncture of her legs—he wanted to spread her there, see if she glistened…

'I am real.'

Her voice, husky, cut through the fever in Sharif's head. His hand tightened around hers and he tugged her towards him. He caught her scent—roses and earth and sand and heat.

The other thing that slammed into his awareness now, up close, was the fact that she was stunningly beautiful—and tall. The top of her head would graze his jaw. Dark eyebrows framed huge almond-shaped eyes. He couldn't make out their colour in the light, but they weren't as dark as his. Straight nose. High cheekbones. That dark olive complexion.

His fingers itched to reach out and touch her, explore to see if her skin felt as satiny as it looked.

But her mouth...

His avid gaze stopped there. Her mouth was beyond provocative. A lush invitation to taste and explore. To crush under his as he enticed her to give up all her secrets.

Sharif felt dizzy. He had met and slept with some of the world's most beautiful women and not one had ever affected him like this. On a visceral, primal level. He knew that if he didn't have this woman—

He couldn't even finish that thought. *He would have her.* He had to.

Her thick, wild hair was wet, but he could see that it was already showing a tendency to curl again.

'Where did you come from?'

A man not remotely prone to superstitions or fantasies, Sharif felt for the first time in his life as if the world around him wasn't entirely...concrete.

'I could ask the same of you.'

The fact that she sounded equally at a loss to explain this set of events was little comfort.

'Does it matter?'

Sharif knew as soon as he asked it that it was a rhetorical question. They were here now. That was all that mattered.

She shook her head. 'No, it doesn't. Who we are doesn't matter either.'

Sharif barely heard the thread of desperation in her voice. It was only afterwards that he would recall it. Long afterwards.

But right now he felt a weight lift off his chest and shoulders. For the first time since he could remember he was with someone who had no idea who he was. There was no preconception, no misconception, no judgement, no expectation.

'Would you like something to eat?'

She blinked. 'Yes…okay. I'd like that.'

Keeping hold of her hand, Sharif led the woman over to his tent.

The tent that was set up in the shelter of the trees was larger than Liyah had expected, but the man still had to duck his head a little to go in. He had to be six foot five at least. Tall enough to make her feel small. And she was used to towering over most people.

Men in particular seemed to find her height a provocation. But not this one. The way he'd looked at her so intently just now… Her heart hadn't slowed down since she'd laid eyes on him.

Her eyes adjusted from the falling light outside to the golden glow of lots of candles. There was a table set up with food, and a place-setting for one. There was a bed in the corner, large and luxurious, with jewel-covered throws.

Liyah looked away quickly, suddenly ambushed by the memory of how it had felt to walk out of the water naked, with his dark gaze on her. She didn't want him to see her looking at the bed. He'd already crossed about a dozen boundaries that, if her rational brain was working, she would never have allowed anyone to cross. Not to mention a complete stranger.

He let her hand go and went over to the chair and pulled it out. 'Please...sit down.'

Liyah looked around. 'There's only one chair.'

'I'll find something. Please.'

It was so surreal that Liyah did as he bade, moving around the table to sit down. She felt him behind her, his hands close to her shoulders. Her hair was still damp. Heavy. It was too long, too unruly, but every time she got frustrated and determined to cut it she would think of the pictures she had of her mother, with the same long hair, and she'd lose the will to let it go.

Any memory or connection with her mother was so tenuous. And precious.

The man had disappeared behind a screen that presumably hid the washing area. And now he reappeared, taking Liyah's breath away with his sheer physicality.

He had put on a plain white T-shirt and it made his dark olive skin look even darker. It highlighted the musculature of his chest, somehow making it more provocative than if he'd still been bare.

He put down a wooden stool on the opposite side of

the table. For the first time she could look at him up close in the light and she was mesmerised.

He was breathtaking. His face was lean and sculpted, the low flickering candlelight casting shadows and making his skin gleam like burnished bronze. Hard jaw defined by stubble. Nose like a blade. Deep-set dark eyes. Fathomless.

His mouth was as strong as the rest of him, but wide. His lips were full, more than hinting at a sensual nature—as if Liyah hadn't noticed that as soon as she'd seen him. He oozed a sexual magnetism that had stunned her as effectively as if he'd shot her with a dart from a gun.

'Are you sure you don't want to take the chair? That doesn't look very comfortable.'

He shook his head and put an empty plate in front of her. 'Help yourself.'

At that moment Liyah realised she was famished. In the stress of the last week she'd barely eaten, and she didn't do well on low food supplies. The food looked... amazing. There was hummus and flatbread. Dolma vine leaves stuffed with meat. Succulent pieces of lamb with balls of spiced rice.

She picked a selection and put them on her plate. She heard a cork and saw him pour white wine into a glass.

He handed it to her. 'Drink?'

Liyah took it, and watched as he poured himself a glass. He raised it. The candles imbued the whole scene with a golden glow that didn't go anywhere near helping her to keep a grasp of reality.

'Here's to...unexpected encounters.'

Liyah lifted her glass. She could feel any desire to try

to restore sanity, to remember who she was, where she was, fatally slipping away, to be replaced by a wholly different and far earthier desire.

She touched her glass to his and it made a low melodic chime. She echoed his words. 'To unexpected encounters.'

He lifted his glass to his mouth, and just before he took a sip he said, 'And what we make of them.'

CHAPTER TWO

'AND WHAT WE make of them.'

Liyah took a sip of her wine as she absorbed that comment. This man was altogether too bold and confident, but he'd woken something inside her. Something equally bold. If not as confident.

'Your eyes are green.'

Liyah looked at him. 'My mother's eyes were green.'

'Try the lamb. It's delicious.'

Liyah picked up a piece of lamb, along with some of the rice, and popped it into her mouth. The meat practically melted on her tongue and the spices in the rice made her taste buds come alive.

'You know this place well.'

It wasn't a question. Liyah swallowed her food and nodded. 'I've always come here. It's usually empty. It doesn't serve as a stopping point as it's so close to the city.' *To the palace.* She pushed her mind away from that reminder.

'Your bird is very tame. How old is he?'

Liyah bit back a smile. *'She.'*

The man smiled and she nearly fell off her chair. It

changed him from being merely stupendously gorgeous to something not of this earth.

'I shouldn't have presumed.'

Liyah recovered her wits. 'She's been mine since I was a child. I trained her out here in the desert.'

'Does she have a name?'

Liyah felt self-conscious. No one had ever cared about her bird except for the falconer at the palace. 'Sheba.'

'Like the Queen? She is a beautiful bird.'

'Yes, she is.'

'Almost as beautiful as her owner.'

Liyah's mouth dried. Her heart thumped. He thought she was beautiful. But she knew that she wasn't really. She was too tall. Her hair was too wild. She couldn't fade gracefully into the background like other women. She always stuck out. Which made her think of her time in Europe. Her dark skin and height had marked her out from the start. Making her a target for people who wanted to exploit her for fun.

Others had told her she was beautiful back then too. And she'd lapped it up, starved of attention and in a new world where she'd felt out of place. But it had been a cruel lie.

This was a timely reminder. She had no idea who this man was and yet she was lapping up his attention like an eager puppy, having learnt nothing.

Liyah put down her napkin and went to stand, but the man caught her hand in his. He was frowning.

'Hey, where are you going?'

'I should leave. I don't know what I was thinking.'

Liyah pulled her hand free. The man stood up.

Just before she got to the opening to the tent, he said, 'Wait. Stop. Please.'

She didn't know him, but she sensed that he didn't say the word *please* much. It sounded rusty. Unused. She stopped and felt him come close behind her.

He said, 'Usually when I compliment a woman she doesn't run away.'

Liyah whirled around, incensed. 'I'm not running away. I've just realised that this is…' She stopped. She didn't even have words for what this was.

He supplied one. 'Crazy?'

'I didn't come here this evening expecting to find… you.'

'And yet here I am. I wasn't expecting company either. Far from it.'

Liyah looked up at him. He was too tall. So broad. He eclipsed everything around him.

'If I wanted to leave now, would you let me?'

He took a step back, looking almost affronted. 'Of course. You're free to go.' But then his expression changed and he said, '*If* you want to. But I don't think you do want to…'

He sounded so sure of himself. Part of Liyah wanted to prove him wrong. She wanted to turn, go outside, pick up her clothes and leave. But a much bigger part of her—the part that had felt little or no compunction about revealing her naked body to him—wanted to stay.

As if sensing her vacillation, he said, 'This thing between us…this connection…is not usual. You do know that?'

Of course she didn't. She'd believed that she'd wanted a man before—*correction, a boy*—but what she'd felt then had been nothing remotely like this swooping exhilarating rollercoaster of sensations. Even the food had tasted more delicious than anything she'd ever tasted before.

Fearing for her very sanity, she almost whispered, 'Are you actually real?'

He took a step towards her again and she could smell him, spicy and musky. He took her hand and lifted it up, placed it on his chest, over his heart.

She felt the strong rhythmic *thump-thump* under her palm. It sent a veritable tsunami of emotions through her. It was so illicitly intimate, yet reassuring at the same time.

Her father ran a conservative household. He didn't approve of displays of affection in public, or in private either. Any physical touch Liyah had experienced growing up had come at the brusque hands of nannies, or the women in the palace hammam.

She'd been in the hammam the day before, and to her eternal shame—because she didn't usually indulge in self-pity—a sense of loneliness and vulnerability had gripped her. She'd found tears running down her face. The only saving grace had been that she'd known they wouldn't be noticed during the ancient full-body-washing ritual.

Tears were a weakness that Liyah rarely indulged in. She had no reason to feel sorry for herself. She'd been born into a privileged world, albeit one that came with responsibilies and duties. She'd had a moment of believing she might escape them—when she'd been in Europe—but deep down she'd always known that her fate was not her own. She just hadn't known how that would mani-fest, or that it would manifest so dramatically.

And yet here she was, with her palm on this man's chest, his heart echoing the drumming of her blood. A sense of fatality gripped her. She had no idea what her husband-to-be was like, or who he was beyond a name—her own stubborn fault for not wanting to know…as if that might stop it happening—but tomor-row she would no longer be *this* anonymous woman.

No longer free to feel the heartbeat of a stranger under her palm. No longer free to swim naked or to take off on her horse when the whim took her. No longer—

'Kiss me, please,' she blurted out, the words rising up from an unstoppable place inside her.

Sharif's blood leapt. He wanted nothing more than to kiss this woman. And a lot more. But he forced himself to stop for a second.

He put his hand over hers on his chest. It felt incred-ibly feminine and delicate. 'Are you sure?'

He had seen the turmoil on her face just now, as if she was agonising. But now it was clear, determined.

She nodded. And said, 'Yes. I'm sure.'

Sharif took his hand from hers and put his hands on her upper arms, tugging her gently towards him until he could feel the heat of her body through the thin robe.

Her hair was already starting to curl wildly again. Her green eyes were huge. Unusual, and adding to her striking beauty. Not many had light-coloured eyes in this region. He wondered again for a second who she might be, but then pushed it aside. It didn't matter. All that mattered was this.

He pulled her closer until he could feel the lush curves of her body come into contact with his. *Dio.* He felt like a schoolboy with his first woman all over again. What the hell was *that* about?

She was looking up at him, both hands splayed on his chest now. Lips parting, trembling slightly, her breath coming in little pants that made her breasts move against him.

He bent his head and covered her mouth with his, and even as a part of him was telling himself that this was no different from any other kiss he knew it was a lie.

Her lips were soft, but firm. Like her. All over. And he'd barely touched her but he was drowning. His hands tightened on her arms as if that would help anchor him as he deepened the kiss and tasted her sweetness.

She was hesitant at first, and that only heightened the eroticism of this relatively chaste kiss, but then she became bolder, matching his exploration with her own, nipping his tongue with her teeth. She wrapped her arms around his neck and came even closer...so close that he could feel the tantalising thrust of her hard nipples through the fabric of their clothes.

He pulled back, dizzy. He needed to see her, feel her. Now.

He must have spoken out loud because she took down her hands and arms and stepped back, dislodging his hold.

And as he watched she pulled his robe up and over her head, and dropped it to the floor of the tent.

He was looking at her as if he'd never seen a woman before. Which was ridiculous, because he had already seen her and she would be an idiot to think for a second that a man like this, who oozed sexuality and confidence, hadn't looked on lots of naked women.

Liyah's mouth felt swollen after that kiss. She could still taste him, dark and explicit, on her tongue.

But that black gaze devoured her now, lingering on her breasts, her belly, her waist. And down to the juncture between her legs. Her thighs.

'Turn around,' he ordered gruffly. .

Liyah did so, welcoming momentary escape from that avid intensity. She heard movement behind her and then felt his heat before she felt him. *He was naked.*

He pulled her hair aside and over one shoulder. His hands came to her arms again and she felt his breath against her before his lips touched her bare skin.

'Okay?' he asked.

His consideration was not something she'd anticipated when she'd behaved so impetuously.

She nodded, and whispered, 'Yes. Please.'

Please keep going. Transport me from this world, from myself, for tonight, so I don't have to—

Liyah sucked in a gasp when the man's arms came under hers and he cupped her breasts in his big hands. His hair-roughened chest was at her back. And she could feel the potency of his hard body. Hard for her.

Heat grew at her core, making her wet. She groaned softly and fell back into him, her legs turning to jelly as one hand left her breast and travelled down, exploring her curves, over her belly to that place between her legs.

He drew her up against him, his erection cupped by her buttocks. With one hand, he explored her breast, fingers finding and trapping her nipple, his other hand gently encouraged her to part her legs, so that he could explore her there. Find the seam of flesh that was the last barrier to the evidence of how much she wanted him. Wanted this.

And then he was there, his fingers opening her up, sinking deep. She clutched at his arm, his hand. Pushing and pulling at the same time. Wanting him to keep doing what he was doing between her legs, but not wanting him to see how much she wanted it.

He whispered against her skin. 'It's okay… I know…'

She gave up fighting her response and opened up even more, allowing him to move his hand between her legs, his fingers seeking and finding and thrusting deep into her clasping flesh.

Liyah might have screamed—she wasn't even sure. All she knew was that he was turning her head so his mouth could fuse with hers as her whole body quivered and shook in his arms, the precursor to the storm he unleashed with a flick of his fingers.

Liyah was floating…and it was only when he laid her down on the bed that she realised she hadn't been floating at all. He'd just carried her over to the bed.

Her whole body was suffused with lingering ecstasy, the waves of orgasm making her inner muscles clench in reaction. She hadn't had an orgasm before…and now she understood.

A wave of gratitude swept through her, and before she could stop herself she said, 'Thank you.'

He came down on the bed beside her, long lean muscles rippling under all that dark skin. 'What for?'

Liyah clamped her mouth shut. She didn't want to admit she hadn't had an orgasm before, despite hav-

ing had sex once. She didn't want to admit that she'd
felt there must be something wrong with her because
she hadn't enjoyed the experience, at all. It had been
humiliating on so many levels and then afterwards—

She shut her mind to that.

She shook her head on the pillow. 'Nothing... Just,
thank you.'

The man smiled.

Liyah bit her lip, wanting his mouth on hers again,
drugging her, transporting her.

To mask her desire, she looked at him. She hadn't
seen his naked body before...he'd been behind her. But
now, as he lay alongside her, she let her gaze move down
over the hard planes of his chest and his taut belly. To
the dark hair between his legs and the rigid length of
his erection. Veins ran up along the shaft, pulsing with
blood. His thighs were thick and muscled.

Liyah felt dizzy, even though she was lying down.
She glanced at him, feeling shy. He was watching her.
She came up on one arm. 'Can I...? Touch you...?'

He lay on his back, his smile turning lazy. Knowing. 'Be my guest.'

Liyah came up on her knees. She tentatively put out
a hand and placed it on his chest, feeling his heart beat
again. It was thumping hard. Fast. She trailed it down
over his belly. His muscles clenched. She looked at him
quickly. He wasn't smiling any more.

He said, 'Go on.'

She was too intimidated by the silk and steel length
of him to explore there just yet, so she traced her fingers
over his thigh, marvelling at the sheer strength. His hips

were narrow, where hers flared out. She'd never been so aware of a man and a woman's innate differences.

His body jerked at her touch, as if tempting her to touch him more intimately.

Her heart-rate leapt and after a moment of hesitation, she gave in to temptation, touching him experimentally.

He made a sound and she stopped.

He looked pained.

She asked, 'What is it?'

'Nothing, just…don't stop.'

Liyah curled her hand around him—as much as she could. There was a drop of moisture at the head and she had the inexplicable urge to lick it, taste his essence. She blushed at the thought.

'Let me see you.'

His voice sounded thick. Not sure what he meant, Liyah looked at him. He sat up slightly, muscles contracting. He took her arms and gently encouraged her to straddle him, placing her so she was spread across his thighs and facing him. Nowhere to hide. Exposed. Her skin prickled with excitement.

His hands moved down to her hips. He sat back against the plumped-up cushions. 'You have beautiful breasts.'

Liyah blushed again. She'd never thought much of her breasts. She'd always been a bit self-conscious of their size, wishing she had a more petite frame like her younger half-sisters. They felt heavy now.

He sat up and cupped them, looking at her briefly before bringing his hot mouth to first one and then the other, teasing her with open kisses and gentle nips on her skin, before placing his mouth where she was screaming internally to be touched.

He sucked one nipple and then the other, tugging at her flesh and making her head fall back at the sensation. He fed her flesh into his mouth as if savouring the most succulent food.

And then, with one hand, he touched her between her legs, where she was so exposed, and without warning she fell over the edge again, gasping in surprise and not a little terrified at this control he could wield so easily over her. It was as if he knew her body better than she did. A stranger.

When her world had stopped spinning she realised that he was lying back and her hands were digging into his chest. He pulled her down so that her breasts were crushed into his chest and then he moved her hair back, finding her mouth and kissing her.

Excitement built again when she felt his erection straining between them. Her body was moving instinctively against his, seeking friction. Seeking *more*.

He expertly manoeuvred her body so that she was sitting up again, poised over him. He held himself in his hand, the head nudging the entrance to her very core. She couldn't breathe. It was as if her body wept with the need to feel him inside her.

She let herself sink onto him slowly as he took his hand away and gripped her hip. He was big. She sucked in a breath but he lay still, letting her dictate the pace as she allowed her body to absorb all that heat and strength.

She held her breath as momentary discomfort made itself felt.

His hands tightened on her hips. 'Are you…?'

She focused on him, her vision blurred by all the sensations coursing through her body. What was he asking? If she was a—?

She shook her head. 'No, I'm not.'

But she'd only had sex once before, and she wasn't even sure if the experience counted, because it had felt nothing like this.

The discomfort had become something else—something much sharper and more pleasurable. Liyah started to move up and down slowly, letting her body get used to his.

They were both breathing heavily now, and Liyah felt sweat sheening her skin. Her movements became faster, and he held her hips lightly, but she could feel the need in him to hold her so that he could take control.

She felt infinitely powerful in that moment. But then her own frustration grew because she couldn't find the perfect rhythm that her body craved.

In a split second he'd manoeuvred them so that she was on her back and he looked down at her, his body still deeply embedded in hers.

He pulled out and her every muscle tensed, waiting for the delicious slide of his body into hers again, but he stopped.

Hoping she didn't sound as desperate as she felt, Liyah said, 'Is something wrong?'

He pulled out fully and her body protested.

'Protection. I have no protection here.'

Liyah didn't understand for a second, and then she did. Relief flowed through her. 'It's okay. I'm on the pill.'

* * *

Sharif looked at the woman under him. Her wild hair was spread around her head. Her skin was flushed dark red, her eyes like bright green jewels. Lips plump.

The effort it had taken him to pull free from the clasp of her body made him shake. No woman—*ever*—had had this effect on him. Sex for him was usually a transitory physical satisfaction. Like scratching an itch. He'd always derived more pleasure out of the chase and the conquest than the actual *act*. He'd always been able to hold himself slightly aloof...

But here—now—that ability to remain aloof was incinerated. He'd almost forgotten his own rule. *Never sleep with a woman without protection*—because he had no intention of revisiting the sins of his father on an innocent child.

In another instant, with another woman, Sharif would have taken this as a wake-up call. His natural cynicism and distrust of people would have flatlined his desire.

But his entire being ached with the need to sheath himself inside her again and throw caution to the wind, following the dictates of his body, mind and soul to seek an oblivion he knew instinctively would eclipse anything he'd felt before.

He didn't even know her name.

He would never see her after this night.

Even more disturbing was this instinct that he had to trust her. Or was that just needy desperation because he wanted her so badly?

'You're on the pill?'

She nodded. 'For over a year now. I wouldn't lie

about something like this. The consequences for someone like me would be…unthinkable.'

Any sliver of sanity that might have pulled Sharif
back from the edge melted into a heat haze. In this moment he believed her—and not just because he wanted to.

He said, 'I'm clean. I got checked recently.'

Even though he never made love without protection.

Her hands went to his chest, palms flat. 'I trust you.'

I trust you.

No women—*no person*—had ever said that to him
before. He had never been in the business of fostering
enough intimacy to invite statements like that. *Until now.*

But he didn't want to dwell on that. Not when every
muscle in his body was screaming with the need to join
his body with this woman's.

He forced himself to say, 'Are you sure?'

She nodded. 'Please—I want this. I want you.'

He found the slick folds that parted, oh, so easily
when he pushed against her, and couldn't help the low
groan of intense satisfaction when he sheathed himself
inside her silky tight embrace again. The fact that this
didn't just feel like *sex* was also something he didn't
want to dwell on.

He forced himself to control his thrusts, letting her
get used to his body. He knew he was big, and he could
tell she was inexperienced—even if she wasn't a virgin.

Gradually he felt her body adjust to his, saw the way
her cheeks flushed a darker pink. The way she bit her
lip. The way she moved under him, lifting her hips. Her
hands explored him, and if she wasn't careful she was
going to push him off the edge way before he was ready.

He caught her hands and raised them above her head,

linking their fingers. He said, 'Spread your legs wider for me.'

She did, and he sank even deeper. She let out a low moan. Sharif let her go and slid his hand under her back, arching her up so that he could find and suck one hard nipple into his mouth, rolling the taut peak before nipping gently.

Her movements became more frenzied, and he felt the telltale flutters along his length as he drove deep and hard. Sweat sheened their skin as they raced to the pinnacle, and it took more control than Sharif had ever had to call on in his life to ensure that she reached it before he did.

She arched up, her whole body taut like a bow, as her orgasm held her high before ripping through her body all the way to her inner muscles, which clenched so hard around Sharif that he was no longer capable of holding back the flood of ecstasy that wiped his brain clean of every single coherent thought.

Today

Liyah woke with a start. She was lying in an unfamiliar bed in unfamiliar surroundings and her body felt…

A rush of heat flashed through her mind when she recalled where she was.

And with whom.

The nameless man.

He was lying on his front beside her, but not touching her. One arm was carelessly hanging over the edge of the bed, the other was bent up over his head. His face was turned to the side, towards her.

Even in sleep he looked fierce. Strong. The stubble lining his jaw was darker...

Her wide awake gaze—tracked down over the sleek muscles, no less impressive at rest. Those narrow hips. His buttocks—firm. A pulse throbbed between her legs when she thought of the sheer power of his body thrusting into hers, so deep she'd seen stars.

A wave of emotion took her by surprise. After her first dismal sexual experience in Europe she'd suspected that there might be something wrong with her. But after last night...

This man had restored a very wounded part of her soul. And her confidence. He'd looked at her as if he'd never seen a woman before. He'd touched her as reverently as if she was infinitely precious, and then he'd made love to her as if he had been starving for something only she could give him.

She'd fallen into a pleasure-induced coma after that first time and had woken in his arms to find him carrying her over to a steaming hot bath that had been hidden behind the screen.

She hadn't even been aware of how tender her muscles were until she'd felt the hot water soothe them. Still stunned after what had happened, she'd been incapable of speech. He'd climbed into the bath behind her, spreading his legs down alongside hers, and had tucked her hair up in a knot before soaping her all over, his big hands making her feel delicate and precious for the first time...*ever.*

She'd turned her head, afraid of the clutch of emotion in her chest—afraid of what it meant and that he'd see it —and had found his mouth. Firm and hot. She'd turned in the bath until she was straddling him, the silky water making it easy to glide over him and sink down onto his erection. The movement of their bodies, as if they'd been made for each other, had quickened as the fever of lust had taken them over, the water splashing all around the tub going unnoticed in their race to find nirvana again.

She had only the vaguest memory of him lifting her out of the bath, rubbing her down briskly with a towel and laying her back down on the bed, of his steely warmth surrounding her, his hand on her breast...

Yet here she was now. Her bones felt liquid.

She noticed, almost lazily, that there were pink trails in the sky outside, just visible above the opening in the tent.

Pink trails heralding dawn.

The dawn of her wedding day.

Suddenly Liyah wasn't feeling lazy any more. Panic gripped her belly. She was due to have henna painted on her hands and feet this morning, in preparation for the afternoon's ceremony.

She had to go. *Now.*

She managed to leave the sumptuous bed without waking him, and stole to the opening of the tent. But there she stopped, giving in to temptation and taking one last look, knowing she'd never see him again. Knowing that she might always wonder if she'd dreamt this night up.

Her eyes devoured his majestic form. Even though he was sprawled in louche splendour across the bed, he was no less impressive or intimidating. His body and his face would be imprinted on her memory. For ever.

That clutch of emotion caught at Liyah again. What

had happened here had been so…unexpected. Unprecedented. And magical. It would be her secret to carry with her, deep inside, where no one would ever find it.

Least of all her new husband.

When Sharif woke his head felt fuzzy, as if he'd had too much to drink. And his body felt pleasantly achy. Heavy. But also light.

But he hadn't had too much to drink.

He'd just had the most intensely erotic experience of his life.

Sharif jacknifed up to sit in the bed as vivid memories assailed him.

But beside him was an empty space. No sign of the wild-haired temptress with the green eyes who had rendered him insensible with desire.

Desire? He grimaced at that. Desire was too ineffectual a word for what he'd felt for her from the moment he'd seen her revealed by the pool.

A wave of lust gripped him as the previous night came back in glorious Technicolor. The way she'd sat astride him, taking him deep into her body, the look of awe on her face, her cheeks darkened with pleasure. And how it had felt when her secret inner muscles had milked him—

Dio. Sharif never dwelled on sex with lovers. He had it—he moved on.

He got out of the bed, feeling dizzy for a moment. Dizzy after a night of unbridled pleasure. He sensed the tent was empty and walked to the entrance, pulling back the material over the opening.

Dawn was bathing the oasis in deep pinks and golds.

Sharif stepped out. Naked. The cool air made his skin prickle, but so did the fact that there was no sign of the woman.

Her horse was gone.

She was gone.

He walked over to the pool. Its serene surface left no hint of the unearthly goddess who had disappeared into its depths only to emerge and prove that she'd been all too earthly.

Sharif's skin prickled even more, and it had nothing to do with the cool air and everything to do with a sense of exposure. Had she in fact existed at all? Or had it been a particularly lurid dream? Was he so jaded that he'd conjured up an erotic fantasy to entertain himself on the eve of his wedding to a woman sight unseen?

In fact the more he thought about it, the more he found it almost easier to believe it hadn't happened. He was no saint, but neither was he inclined to 'instalust' or casual sex with a stranger. Usually his women were carefully vetted.

Not that it stopped them from crying to the tabloids when he ended their liaisons, a snide inner voice reminded him.

He ignored the voice. And then went cold as he thought of something else. They hadn't used protection. He'd taken her at her word when she'd mentioned being on the pill.

He shook his head. It couldn't have happened. He *never* indulged in unprotected sex. A man like him was a magnet for women who wanted to secure their lives by having his baby. And he was not in the market for babies. Not now. Not ever.

In a bid to wake himself out of this reverie and come back to sanity, Sharif stepped into the water and dived deep into its inky depths. The shock of the water made his brain freeze, and only when his lungs were ready to burst did he come back up to the surface.

As he sucked in deep breaths his mind cleared. It *had* been a dream. Lurid and very real, yes, but a dream. That was the only way he could explain it. And he always had crazy dreams when he was in the desert. Admittedly, never like that...

Sharif walked out of the water, a sense of almost relief coursing through him. Relief that it hadn't been real, but also a tinge of regret. But of course she hadn't been real—a woman like that couldn't possibly be...

Just then something caught his peripheral vision. Something white. He went over to it. It was near the shoreline, on the ground.

Sharif stooped down and picked it up. A scrap of material. White. Cotton. Plain. Underwear.

A flash of memory came back to him—the woman stepping out of her clothes. Diving into the water.

She *had* been real.

The relief that coursed through him made a mockery of his assurance that it had all been a dream, but Sharif's mouth firmed. It might have been real, and he might have acted completely out of character, but she was gone now, like a ghost, and she would have to remain that way. Within a few hours he was to marry a woman he'd never met. He didn't need the distraction of an erotic temptress.

It was time to avenge his mother's betrayal and her death, and nothing would get in his way.

CHAPTER THREE

'YOUR WIFE MAY now reveal her face.'

Liyah's heart was thumping so hard she was surprised no one else could hear it. It had taken off like a racehorse, obliterating the escalating dread, the minute she'd seen her husband-to-be and recognised him as her nameless lover from the previous night.

No longer nameless.

He was Sheikh Sharif Bin Noor Al Nazar. Or, as he was better known in America and Europe, Sharif Marchetti, CEO of a vast luxury conglomerate.

This information had been supplied to her by the gossiping women at the henna painting ceremony earlier that day, while there had also been mention of how handsome he was.

Liyah's head had been too full of the previous night to take much notice.

He was resplendent in Al-Murja royal dress, which made him look even taller and broader. The cream silk of his royal robes, with gold thread piping, enhanced his dark skin tone. He wore no headdress. But Liyah noticed that his hair had been trimmed since last night. And his jaw was clean-shaven.

She remembered the graze of his stubble against her inner thighs…

She slammed a door on that incendiary memory.

The shock that had hit her like a body-blow as soon as she'd recognised him still gripped her, keeping her in a sort of paralysis. The only thing that had given her the time to absorb that shock was the fact that he hadn't yet recognised *her*. But he was about to…

The women came forward—her sister Samara was one of her attendants today—and they deftly and far too quickly removed the elaborate face shield that was a traditional part of weddings in Taraq, and had been for hundreds of years.

Liyah blinked as her eyes adjusted to the brightness of the throne room in the royal palace. A grand description for what was really a modest fortress.

She looked up at her husband with dread lining her belly and saw the expressions chase across his face as if in slow motion. Recognition. Confusion. And then shock, disbelief. Anger.

And then his mouth opened and he uttered one word. *'You!'*

Somehow—miraculously—no one seemed to have caught Sharif's exclamation of recognition, and the ceremony finished as Liyah's hand was placed over his— the moment when she was deemed to be his wife.

Her hand was covered in the dark, intricate stains of henna. The red swirls swam a little in front of her eyes and she had to suck in a breath, terrified she might faint. The heavy robes and headdress she wore weren't helping.

Her gaze had slid away from his as soon as he'd spoken, but she could feel those dark eyes on her, boring into her, silently commanding her to look at him.

She felt numb, and she welcomed it, because if the numbness wore off then she knew she would be subjected to an onslaught of sensations and memories.

When she'd returned to the palace earlier, and undergone the pre-wedding bathing ritual, she'd lamented her mystery lover's touch and smell being washed from her body, even though she knew how inappropriate it would have been to go to another man while his imprint was still on her.

But he was no longer a mystery. He was her husband. And that fact filled her with so many conflicting feelings that she felt dizzy all over again.

They were led in a procession with the guests and both families into another formal room. The ballroom. Where a lavish feast had been laid out.

Normally weddings in Taraq would be three and four-day affairs—but, as her father had told her, this was to be a much briefer celebration.

Liyah and Sharif were seated at the top table, side by side. She took her hand from his and sat down, studiously avoiding looking to her right, where he sat. The ring that had been placed on her finger during the ceremony felt heavy. She'd barely looked at it—a thick, ornate gold ring, with a bluish stone in a circular setting surrounded by diamonds.

The King of Al-Murja, a man as tall and dark and handsome as Sharif, sat nearby, looking austere. As austere as her husband.

Husband. She felt dizzy again, even though she was sitting down.

Liyah cursed herself now for not having looked him up. If she had, she would have known who he was at the oasis.

And would that have changed her behaviour?

Liyah couldn't say how she would have reacted last night even if she'd known who he was. It was all too much to process.

And then, from her right, came a low and steely tone. 'Look at me, *wife*.'

Liyah gulped and slowly turned her head to meet those far too memorable dark eyes. She noticed now that there were gold rings around his irises. So not totally dark. Golden. Molten.

'So what was that last night? Were you trying out the wares before you committed to marriage with a stranger? Should I be flattered you deemed me suitable?'

His voice was cold enough to make her shiver—a big difference from how he'd sounded last night. The mid-Atlantic twang mocked her now. As did her instinct last night that he was not just *anyone*.

'No,' she croaked. 'It wasn't like that. I had no idea who you were.'

He made a rude sound. 'I find that hard to believe.'

His accusing tone broke Liyah out of her shocked paralysis. 'Wait… Did you know who I was?'

'No.'

A dart of hurt lanced her. He'd been equally disinclined to know about her. But she shouldn't be surprised—after all her sister had told her. *He just wants a wife. He doesn't care who that is.*

'Then I could accuse you of the same—maybe you

did know who I was and you wanted to make sure *I* was suitable.'

'You weren't a virgin. That would make you very unsuitable to some.'

Liyah flushed at that. In this part of the world he would be within his rights to reject her on those grounds... Except the time to do it would have been the moment he'd recognised her.

'Are you going to say something?' Liyah immediately thought of the potential repercussions for her younger sister, who might be denied the husband she wanted to punish Liyah.

But Sharif shook his head slowly. 'No. I'm not a hypocrite. I'm far from a virgin. I don't expect my wife to be. Anyway, that's not what this marriage will be about.'

Liyah looked at him. She frowned. 'What's that supposed—?'

But she was cut off when the music started, drowning out what she'd been about to say. She had to face forward to watch the traditional dancers.

Her brain was racing, wanting to know what Sharif had meant. She cursed herself again for not having looked him up. She would have been better prepared. But it was too late to dwell on regrets. Or on reckless decisions made in the heat of the moment.

She'd never expected to see him again but now he was her husband. And she would have to deal with the consequences.

Sharif's blood was boiling as he sat beside his brand-new wife. Aaliyah. She now had a name. The woman who had driven him senseless with lust only a few hours

ago. The same woman he'd suspected of being a fig-
ment of his imagination.

He didn't believe for a second that she hadn't known
who he was last night. It was too conveniently serendipitous that she'd just happened to visit the oasis when
he'd been there.

Someone must have told her that he hadn't arrived
at the palace with his entourage. And she'd come to
investigate her future husband. The thought that she'd
been laughing at him the whole way through the marriage ceremony, behind her veil, set his nerves on edge.

Little happened in Sharif's life that he wasn't in control of. And this was not how he'd envisaged his marriage starting—with his blood boiling over with shock,
anger and, even worse, *lust*.

Even though her body was now covered in the voluminous red and white traditional wedding robes of
Taraq, Sharif could picture every dip and hollow. How
she'd looked when she'd stepped out of the water in
front of him, water sluicing down over endless curves
and gleaming skin. The long sleek limbs. Her breasts,
perfectly shaped and heavy…the juncture between her
legs where dark hair curled enticingly, inviting him to
explore—

Dio. He'd planned on making the most of his wife
in the coming weeks, having her by his side at as many
events as possible to ensure that the Marchetti Group
brand was at its most stable and valuable for when he
put his plans into motion.

By his side. Not in his bed. And most definitely *not*
under his skin.

The last woman in the world he'd ever expected to

see again, who he wanted nowhere near him, was in fact now his wife. And as his wife, she would be in close proximity at all times. Whether he liked it or not.

'Liyah…you look so sophisticated. I've never seen you like this.'

Liyah grimaced at her reflection in the mirror. The shift dress and matching jacket were in pastel pink. She hated pink. She hated anything too girly and always had, preferring a far more relaxed and casual tomboy aesthetic.

She'd barely even taken notice of the women who had measured her up the day after her father had allowed her to take Samara's place as Sharif's bride. She'd been too impatient to see her horse, whom she hadn't seen in months, while she'd been in Europe.

But now she knew why she'd been measured up.

Because her…her *husband* had provided this going-away outfit. And another bag containing a change of clothes, sleepwear, underwear and toiletries.

She thought she looked ridiculous. Her hair was too wild and unruly for an outfit like this, but it was too late to try and tame it. And, even worse, suddenly she felt nervous. She'd managed to avoid Sharif while the reception had been underway and they'd been surrounded by a hundred people, but now she would be stepping onto a plane with him and there would be nowhere to hide.

'My hair…my hair is too much.'

Samara stepped up behind her and pulled her hair back into a low ponytail. 'Your hair is beautiful, Liyah, like the rest of you.'

Samara rested her chin on Liyah's shoulder and she

met her sister's dark gaze in the mirror. Liyah didn't even share the same eye colour as her siblings. She really was the cuckoo in the nest.

Samara's pretty face was serious. 'Thank you, Liyah, for what you've done. You have no idea how much—'

A rising swell of emotion made Liyah turn around. She clasped her sister close before the emotion became too much to push down. 'I know,' she whispered. 'I know. Just be happy, Sammy, okay? Marry Javid and be happy.'

At that moment Liyah truly wished for her sister that she wouldn't be disappointed by love. Or destroyed by it, like their father.

Her sister nodded against her. She pulled back, dark eyes bright with tears. But she forced a smile. 'I'll miss you.'

'And I'll miss you. But call me any time, okay?'

Samara nodded again.

Maids entered to take Liyah's bags down to where her husband waited in the royal courtyard and Liyah followed them. Samara was the only one who had come to say goodbye. Liyah hated it that it still hurt. That some small vulnerable part of her had still hoped that she'd be important to her family. To her father.

She stopped in the shadows just under the massive stone archway that led outside. Sharif was pacing back and forth. He saw the maids coming out with the bags and flicked his wrist to look at his watch, clearly impatient. But Liyah couldn't move.

Gone were the elaborate gold and cream robes of the regal Sheikh—and gone was the wild nameless man who had seduced her into a place of heated insanity last night. In their place was another incarnation…this one even more intimidating.

His tall, lean body was sheathed in an immaculate three-piece dark suit. A white shirt, open at the neck, highlighted his dark skin. He *should* have looked more civilised. More urbane. But if anything he looked even more elemental. Wild. Dangerous.

Even though she'd slept with him, she felt in that moment that she'd never truly know him, and a little shiver skated over her skin. A kind of premonition that as soon as she stepped out of this shadow and into the sunlight, under his gaze and his protection, her life would never be the same. And she knew it wouldn't—for obvious reasons, and also for much deeper and more secret reasons that she really did not want to investigate right now.

The self-protective walls she'd cultivated her whole life suddenly felt very flimsy.

The sun was setting, bathing everything with a golden glow. It had been around this time yesterday that Liyah had left the palace to ride out to the oasis.

Suddenly, in spite of everything, she had a sense that she didn't regret what had happened at the oasis. It had been too earth-shattering to regret. It had changed something inside her.

A man who looked like an aide hurried over to Sharif's side, and Liyah heard Sharif speak in a low, harsh tone.

'Find her.'

Steeling herself, Liyah stepped forward out of the shadows. 'I'm here. Ready to go.'

* * *

Sharif turned around, his whole body reacting with a jolt of awareness just to hearing her husky voice.

Damn.

She had changed out of the traditional wedding robes that dated back to when her family had been Bedouin nomads. Sharif had asked an assistant to ensure she received appropriate clothes for her transition into his world as his wife, but clearly he hadn't researched much about her, or what she looked like.

Nor did you, reminded an inner voice.

He quashed the sting of his conscience when he thought of how little it had registered when he'd been asked if he would mind marrying the eldest Princess of Taraq and not her sister.

He'd agreed, and in the same instant moved on to the next item on his agenda—because it really didn't matter to whom he was married. All he needed was a wife.

But now he was aware of the significance of having chosen another woman, however carelessly.

Would the other sister have been sent to the oasis to seduce him, too?

The pastel pink did nothing for her skin tone, and the plain design of the dress effectively hid the spectacular curves that he couldn't stop seeing in his mind's eye. All he could think about was the fact that this woman needed to be dressed in bold and vibrant colours. With jewels at her throat and ears. Her wrists. Arms. And with silk and satin clinging to every luscious inch of her body.

Nothing could really detract from her sheer luminous beauty, though. Not even her unstyled pulled-back hair, or the fact that her face was scrubbed clean. Sharif couldn't recall the last time a woman had made so little effort for him.

Irritation at his reaction to her and this whole situation, which had morphed beyond what he'd expected, made his voice sharp. 'We should leave. My plane is waiting at the airfield.'

He noticed how she lifted her chin at his tone and something flashed in those stunning green eyes. A flash of defiance. His blood sizzled and he gritted his jaw.

He ignored his driver standing to attention and opened the back door of the Jeep himself. 'Please.'

He'd said *please* more than he'd ever said it in his life within the past twenty-four hours.

Aaliyah moved forward, the nude high heels making her legs look even longer and more lissom, reminding him of how strong her thighs were. Firm and lean from riding her thoroughbred stallion to deserted oases so she could swim naked and tempt men. Tempt *him*.

Suddenly the thought that he might not have been the only one to see her like that made his blood spike to dangerous levels.

He gritted his jaw even harder as her clean, unmanufactured scent tickled his nostrils as she got into the car and her dress slid up, revealing a taut and silky-smooth thigh. He'd noticed that the heels put her tantalisingly closer to his mouth too.

He closed the door and walked around the vehicle to get into the front beside the driver. The sooner they were back in his world, on his turf, where he could regain some sense of control, the better.

* * *

Liyah woke with a start, not sure were she was. There was a voice.

'Mrs Marchetti?'

Who was Mrs Marchetti?

It came again, insistent, along with a peremptory knock on wood.

She was on her husband's private jet.

It all came rushing back.

'Mrs Marchetti? We're landing in half an hour.'

Liyah sat up in the bed. The voice was on the other side of the bedroom door. 'Thank you. I'm awake,' she croaked out.

'Would you like some breakfast?'

Liyah saw the pink trails across the sky outside. They'd chased the dawn from the Middle East to the west.

'Just some coffee would be lovely, thank you.'

She was about to land in a whole new world and life. She'd expected this to be happening with a stranger. Well, he still was a stranger. But one she knew intimately.

Liyah saw the en suite bathroom and went in, groaning when she saw the frizz ball her hair had become. Her face was creased too, from where she'd lain down. She felt sticky.

She noticed that someone had left her bags in the bedroom and took the opportunity to freshen up, pulling out a pair of dark trousers and a long-sleeved cashmere top. Simple, elegant. Better than the powder-pink dress.

She took a quick shower, tying her hair up out of the

way. It was too much of a job to get into washing and drying it now.

When she'd dried off and changed, she found a mercifully flat pair of shoes and took a breath and went into the cabin.

She could see Sharif's dark head over his seat-back. When she came closer he was engrossed in his laptop. He glanced at her as she came alongside him and slid into the seat on the other side of the aisle. She only realised then that she'd left her hair in a knot on the top of her head, too wild to let loose.

The steward came over with a steaming coffee and Liyah smiled her thanks, accepting it gratefully, hoping she didn't look too dishevelled.

She took a sip, relishing the hot tart taste, and then risked another look at Sharif. He closed his laptop and she noticed stubble on his jaw. He'd taken off his jacket but still wore the waistcoat of the suit. Shirtsleeves rolled up. He was utterly civilised and *un*civilised all at the same time. A potent mix.

'Did you work all night?'

He accepted a coffee from the steward too. He looked at her, arching a brow. 'Concerned about me, Aaliyah?'

His voice made her insides tighten with awareness. This man was so dangerous. And he already knew so much about her. Too much.

Up until the cataclysmic moment when she'd realised who her husband was, she'd felt safe in the knowledge that her uncharacteristic behaviour would never be scrutinised in the cold light of day. But the universe was laughing at her now. Not only would her behaviour be scrutinised, but she'd married a man whose only im-

pression of her was based on the illicit night they'd
shared together. And she had no defence. She'd been
bolder and more brazen than at any other time in her
life.

'Don't call me Aaliyah. It's Liyah. Please.'

'Liyah, then.' His gaze dropped, taking in her change
of clothes. 'Dark matte colours and pinks do nothing
for you,' he observed. 'We'll remedy that. I have lots
of events lined up that you'll be required to attend by
my side.'

Liyah flushed at the way he assessed her so coolly,
as if she was some kind of mannequin. Feeling defensive she said, 'I didn't choose the clothes. They were
picked for me.'

'Well, you didn't offer any information on what you
preferred,' Sharif pointed out.

Liyah said nothing, because she had scant interest in
fashion or trends, and she wasn't sure she would have
been adept at knowing what *did* suit her. The fact that
she suspected this man did made her feel defensive all
over again. She really knew next to nothing about him.

'My father said you control a…a luxury conglomerate?'

His dark gaze narrowed on her face. She felt very
bare. Not that she was used to wearing make-up, but
she'd like some kind of armour right now.

'Yes, I run it with my two half- brothers.'

So, he had family. Liyah absorbed that.

Sharif frowned. 'You really didn't know who I was
at the oasis?'

She shook her head. 'I figured there would be plenty

of time to learn about who you were. After all, we're married now, for better or worse. For a long time.'

'You weren't much interested in the prenuptial agreement. My staff told me you only glanced through it before signing.'

Liyah shrugged. 'I thought that would please you?'

'It intrigues me. I don't know a woman who wouldn't have gone through the document with a team of lawyers and dissected it to within an inch of its life before engaging in negotiatons for the maximum they could get their hands on.'

'The women you know don't sound very nice.'

A muscle in his jaw ticked. 'That could very well be the case, but as one of the wealthiest people on the planet I do tend to attract a certain type. So what makes you different? I know you don't have your father's fortune to fall back on, because your family is all but bankrupt—like your country. Hence the eagerness to marry you, or anyone, off.'

Liyah blinked. 'So it's true…the rumour about the fiscal debt in Taraq?'

Sharif nodded. 'Your father and his ministers have overextended themselves hugely in redeveloping the country.'

Liyah had heard the rumours—especially when she'd been abroad—but hadn't known if they were true or not. Naturally her father would never share such information with her. Not even when she was helping dig her own country out of debt with this marriage.

'I don't depend on my father for an income or an inheritance,' Liyah said. 'He wrote me out of the family will long ago.'

'Why?'

'Because my mother left an inheritance to me, her only child. My father couldn't touch it, and I inherited when I was eighteen. It's probably nothing compared to the wealth you command, but it's enough to keep me secure.'

'That's the only thing you checked in the prenup—to make sure that our marriage didn't give me any rights over the money you have independently.'

Liyah nodded. 'So I don't need anything from you.'

An expression crossed his face, too fast to decipher, but Liyah thought it was scepticism.

He said, 'That's refreshing to know. But let me know how you feel when I initiate our divorce and you've become used to a life of comfort and luxury beyond your wildest dreams.'

'Divorce?' They'd only just got married.

'You really should have read that prenuptial agreement properly. It's all in there. When you signed the contract, the day before the wedding—hours before we met at the oasis—you agreed to a divorce at the earliest in six months and at the latest in a year's time. This is a marriage in name only—purely for appearances.'

Liyah let this sink in. She should be feeling relief right now, at the thought that not only was this a marriage in name only but that it was also to be shortlived. But what she was feeling was more ambiguous. Curiosity...

'Why such a specific timeframe?'

'Because I only need a wife until such time as I don't need one any more. Once certain...objectives have been met.'

The air steward approached them again, to inform

them that they'd be landing any minute and to ask them to make sure they were buckled in.

Liyah's head was buzzing with this information. If what Sharif was saying was true, then within a year at the most she'd have her freedom again. And by that time Samara would be married into her new family, so Liyah wouldn't have any reason to return to a place that had never really welcomed her. She really would be free.

So why didn't that induce joy?

The wedding ring on Liyah's finger felt very heavy all of a sudden, and she twisted it absently on her finger.

Sharif asked sharply, 'Does it not fit?'

Liyah looked at him. She shook her head. 'It fits fine…it's just…*big*.'

The plane touched down smoothly at that moment. As the roar of the throttle eased, and the plane made its way to the hangar where they would disembark, Liyah asked, 'This really was always intended to be a marriage in name only?'

Sharif nodded. 'As per the prenuptial agreement— it's all there in black and white.'

'But what…?' Liyah stopped, suddenly hesitant.'

Sharif lifted a brow. 'What…?'

Liyah could feel herself getting hot again. 'What about the fact that we…?' She stopped again, unable to articulate the words.

'Slept together?'

She nodded.

Sharif's expression hardened. 'That was a mistake. It won't happen again. This marriage isn't about that.'

Liyah couldn't look away from Sharif's hard expression. *'It won't happen again.'* A word trembled on her tongue. *Why?* But she stopped herself from letting it slip out, cursing herself for not realising sooner.

She'd been inexperienced. He hadn't. Clearly what had been a transformative experience for her had not been nearly as earth-shattering for him, and she felt mortified now for assuming otherwise.

She should be welcoming this development. The fact that he didn't really want a wife. He'd seduced her so easily. She'd lain down and bared her entire body and soul to him. She'd behaved totally out of character. Did she really want to risk revealing herself to him again? *No.*

The plane had come to a stop now, and staff were opening doors. Liyah gathered her things and avoided Sharif's eye, terrified that he might read something she couldn't hide.

Disappointment.

CHAPTER FOUR

ABOUT AN HOUR after they'd landed at the airfield Sharif watched Liyah walk around the vast space of his penthouse. A helicopter had brought them from the airfield to the building Sharif owned, where he had an apartment at the very top.

Liyah had looked mesmerised as they'd flown over the iconic city.

'Have you been to New York before?' he'd asked her.

She'd just shaken her head, eyes wide and glued to the canopy of tall sparkling buildings below. It had made Sharif look down too, for the first time in a long time. Normally he was in such a hurry to get to the next place, next meeting...

Now she walked through the vast open living space, and Sharif noted it dispassionately through her eyes. Impeccably decorated, with a neutral background of varying shades of grey. The furniture was sleek and elegant—antique. Works of art, on the walls and dotted around the room on tables, provided pops of colour and texture.

It struck him now that he'd never really felt fully connected with this space. He had no more attachment to this apartment than he did to any hotel suite.

Massive curtains were pulled back from floor-to-ceiling windows and a huge set of French doors that led out to a terrace overlooking Central Park. Liyah stood at the window and looked out.

Her hair was still up in a messy knot. The trousers and top she'd changed into did little to hide her body. She could be a model, with her height and proportions. But, her generous curves would put her in the plus size bracket —which was ridiculous, Sharif knew, because she was a perfectly healthy weight.

It was an aspect of the fashion industry that was slowly changing to reflect a far more accurate depiction of women's bodies, and not before time.

He didn't welcome the hum of electricity that seemed to have become a permanent fixture in his blood since she'd been revealed at the wedding. *Since last night.* He defended himself. She was truly stunning, even as pared back as she was right now. And he was only human. He'd always appreciated a beautiful woman.

But something prickled over Sharif's skin as he contemplated what a knockout she would be when she was dressed to impress. He had a feeling that she would easily transcend the most beautiful women he'd ever seen. And he inhabited a world where beauty wasn't just a given. It was expected. Demanded.

He resolved to speak to his team about making sure there were no skeletons in her closet that might derail his plans. But he was sure there weren't. The Mansour royal family weren't renowned for creating headlines—

which was one of the reasons he'd decided to make the most of the diplomatic marriage.

Liyah was still trying to get her bearings after the helicopter ride that had whisked them over to the island of Manhattan, to this tall, gleaming spire of steel where they'd landed on the roof. She looked over the expanse of Central Park nearby—less lush than usual at this time of year, in late winter, but still beautiful.

A tiny bubble of hysteria rose inside her as she realised that it was no wonder she couldn't get her bearings. Her feet had literally hardly touched the ground since they'd landed. And was this how her new husband lived? In the clouds? Far above the mere mortals below? He probably got whatever was the opposite of a head rush if he had to go down to ground level.

She could feel him behind her, albeit a few feet away. Looking at her. Was he trying to figure her out? Or was she so inconsequential to him that she wasn't even worth that?

She turned around and felt an immediate rush of awareness when she found that he *was* looking at her. Hands in pockets. Supremely at home against this luxurious backdrop. She might be from a royal family but she knew that whatever riches and privileges she'd grown up with could never have prepared her for *this* world. They were at another level now. Literally. He could probably buy and sell her entire country a few times over and still have change.

Liyah folded her arms, feeling self-conscious. 'If you don't mind me saying, you look as if you were doing just fine without a wife.'

Sharif moved then, with a fluid athletic grace that made Liyah's mouth go dry. He took off his jacket and draped it gracefully over a chair and then sat down on a couch, his large body all at once relaxed and yet alert. Primed. He had a stillness about him that was seriously unnerving, but also mesmerising. Like a predator that looked benign until it struck with deadly precision.

He put out a hand, 'Please, sit—make yourself at home.'

Liyah's mouth compressed as she took in the vast array of sumptuous couches and chairs covered in smooth soft velvet. Tactile and yet intimidating. Because they looked as if they'd never been touched. She chose an armchair at a right angle to his couch and sat gingerly.

Sharif said, 'I can assure you that I do indeed need a wife at this particular juncture. But tell me something… why did you offer yourself up in your sister's place?'

The thought that he could be here right now with Samara and not *her* sent a dark shard of something very disturbing deep into Liyah's gut. *Jealousy?*

Liyah felt prickly after that disturbing revelation. 'Samara is only nineteen.'

'Which, as you know, in Taraq and Al-Murja is a perfectly respectable age to get married.'

Liyah responded stiffly. 'I just think it's too young to throw away your independence.'

Sharif raised a brow. His mouth quirked. 'I've married a feminist?'

'Is that a problem?'

Sharif laid an arm across the back of the couch and it pulled the material of his shirt and waistcoat across his broad chest. Distracting Liyah. She cursed him, because he probably knew exactly what he was doing.

He answered, 'Not at all. I don't see how any woman can say she's *not* a feminist.'

Liyah's prickliness and scattered thoughts disappeared. She looked at him.

He said, 'Don't look so surprised. My mother was a strong woman, and if it hadn't been for her I would have had to spend even more time with my father.'

'How old were you when she died?'

Sharif didn't move a muscle, but Liyah sensed his reticence.

'Nine. It was a long time ago.'

Clearly they'd been close. Liyah felt a pang to think of how different her own life might have been if her mother hadn't died so young.

'So,' he repeated, 'why did you take your sister's place?'

Liyah hesitated at the prospect of telling Sharif the truth, but then reminded herself that he hadn't even cared which sister he married. 'Because she's in love with someone else and wants to marry him.'

'But you just said you think she's too young to give up her independence…isn't it a contradiction to approve of her marrying someone else?'

Liyah's conscience pricked. She *had* just contradicted herself—spectacularly. She felt like squirming. No one had ever questioned her this closely about anything. 'I just want her to be happy… But I'm afraid she'll be disappointed. Because love doesn't exist—or, if it does, it's a destructive force.'

'That's a very cynical view to have.'

'Something tells me that a man who is prepared to seduce a stranger the night before his arranged marriage doesn't exactly hold love in high esteem,' Liyah observed drily.

Sharif acknowledged that with a dip of his head. 'Touché.'

For a moment Liyah felt a heady rush of exhilaration. Here was a kindred spirit. Was that why she'd been so drawn to him on sight? Because she'd sensed an unconscious affinity? It would certainly help explain her uncharacteristic behaviour.

And yet, even though she recognised and welcomed the sense of affinity, the exhilaration faded to leave a hollow echo inside her to know he was as cynical as her.

'So, who hurt you?'

Liyah's breath stopped for a second at his question. She wondered if she'd heard correctly. 'Excuse me?'

'You're not innocent, but you're not experienced. So, whoever your lover was, he either hurt you badly enough to spark your cynicism or he merely confirmed it. And he didn't ensure that you were satisfied.'

Liyah wanted to slide under the chair and into the floor. Had it been so obvious? No wonder he didn't want to repeat the experience.

'You think you see a lot.'

He practically smirked. 'I know I do. It is a skill honed over many years.'

The need to know how and why he'd developed such a skill hovered on Liyah's tongue, but before she could say a word there was a sound and they both blinked, as if taken by surprise at the way their conversation had engrossed them.

Liyah looked to the door, where a middle-aged gentleman stood. She hadn't even known anyone else was in the place, but it was so vast she wasn't surprised.

Sharif stood up. 'Liyah, I'd like you to meet Thomas Burke, the house manager here.'

Liyah stood up and met the man halfway. Shaking his hand, she smiled, feeling suddenly shy.

'Mrs Marchetti, it's a pleasure to welcome you to New York.'

Sharif glanced at his watch and said, 'I have to go downtown for some meetings and to catch up on my calls. Thomas will show you around and take note of any dietary requirements. You should settle in, Liyah, I'll be back for dinner.'

'Take note of any dietary requirements.' As if she was literally an employee.

Which she pretty much was.

Sharif walked out, taking his jacket with him, and Liyah breathed out fully for the first time since they'd arrived at the apartment.

She dutifully followed Thomas around the different rooms and tried not to let her jaw drop too obviously. There were two dining rooms—informal and formal. A massive kitchen with its own elegant dining area. There was a gym, with a lap pool, and a media centre, complete with a cinema that could seat about fifty people.

There were numerous bedrooms.

She noticed that Thomas didn't show her into Sharif's, but she was given a room just across the hall and it was show-stopping. Decorated in dark blues and greys, with a shag pile carpet, it was decadent and glamorous.

It had its own terrace and a dressing room, and en

suite bathroom that was about as big as the hammam back in Taraq.

Thomas stood in the doorway, not a hint of curiosity about the fact that the new Mrs Marchetti and her husband were obviously not traditional man and wife showing on his face.

'As Mr Marchetti said, let me know if you have any specific dietary preferences and I'll pass them on to the chef.'

The chef!

Liyah balked. 'How many staff are here?'

Thomas calculated for a second. 'Daily, about three—the housemaid, the chef and myself. Then weekly there's a few more—the florist…people like that.'

Liyah had seen the gorgeous colourful blooms in the hall… Thomas was looking at her. She hadn't answered. 'Oh, sorry—nothing. No preferences. I eat anything.'

Thomas looked almost comically taken aback for a moment, and then he bowed ever so slightly and smiled. 'Very good. Dinner will be served at seven, and Mr Marchetti will be in the lounge for an aperitif at six-thirty. Just press the bell by your bed if you need anything in the meantime.'

Thomas left and Liyah investigated her space. Her luggage had been magically unpacked and put away, and she tried not to wince at how shabby her things looked in the pristine space.

She had sisters who wouldn't be caught dead in anything without a designer label, but that had just been one of the many differences between them and Liyah.

She explored the terrace, taking in the truly stupendous view. The sidewalk looked many miles below her, where people scurried like ants. The sky was bright blue and the air was sharp and cold. But there was no snow.

Liyah had never seen snow. It hadn't ever been that cold when she'd been in Europe.

Despite her sleep on the plane, Liyah felt weary. It had been a tumultuous couple of days. And this was supposedly her wedding night with her new husband. Except it was morning—daytime—and they were on the other side of the world. And he obviously had no intention of sleeping with her again.

Thoroughly discombobulated, and not wanting to dwell on the revelations of her new situation, Liyah took off her clothes and crawled into the enormous bed between sheets that felt like silk to the touch. She was asleep in seconds.

That evening Sharif looked out over the view of a low-ering grey sky. He'd never really got used to the cold winters in New York, but as this was where he'd moved the headquarters of the Marchetti Group's operations after his father's death he'd come to tolerate them.

Moving here from the main hub in Rome had been his first step in breaking all ties with his father's legacy. His first step in stamping out his father's influence. The next steps would be the final death knells and would wipe Domenico Marchetti's name out of existence, reducing his legacy to dust.

But even now, as he reminded himself of all that was at stake and all that was to come, Sharif couldn't focus. He was distracted. He'd been distracted all day. Thinking of *her*. His new wife. The woman who was also his mysterious temptress from the oasis—who had lured him like a siren and then kissed him like a novice.

But now he knew better. She'd been no novice.

She'd known exactly what she was doing at that oasis and she'd taken him for a complete fool—

A sound from behind him brought his thoughts to a stop. He turned around slowly. His wife stood in the doorway. She looked hesitant. She was wearing a long cream traditional Taraqi tunic. V-necked, it dipped just low enough to show the top of the curve of her breasts. She also wore slim-fitting matching trousers and flat sandals. He noticed there was still henna on her feet. If this was a traditional marriage he would be taking her to his bed tonight.

A skewer of need twisted in Sharif's gut and he crushed it. This was *not* a traditional marriage and he would *not* be taking her to his bed. Ever again.

Her hair was down, curling wildly around her shoulders, parted in the middle to reveal the effortless beauty of her face. Those huge almond eyes. Wide, generous mouth, lush lips. High cheekbones.

Sharif could imagine her as a teenager, all coltish limbs and awkward grace. But now she was a grown woman, and he had seriously underestimated her.

'Would you like a drink?' He forced civility into his voice when he felt far from civil.

She nodded and walked in.

Sharif couldn't help but notice the soft sway of her breasts under the material of her tunic. *Dio.* She wasn't wearing a bra. Considering what he knew now, he suspected that was on purpose. Her talk of not needing money from him had been a cute deflection from her true nature.

'A soda and lime would be nice, thank you.'

So demure. So deceptive.

Sharif poured her drink, handed it to her, and then poured himself a Scotch.

She hovered, as if unsure what to do or where to go.

Her apparent reticence irritated him now. It was all an act. He cursed himself for not investigating her sooner. But he *had* investigated her sister, and nothing untoward had come back, so he'd just assumed she would be the same. A serious lapse in Sharif's usual attention to detail.

'Please, sit, Liyah. You don't need permission.'

Liyah sat on one of the couches, sending him a slightly inquisitive look, which he ignored.

Sharif chose a chair. Instead of demanding that she explain herself straight away, he decided to play dumb. 'Did you rest this afternoon?'

She nodded and took a sip of her drink. 'Yes, thank you.'

But Sharif knew he couldn't string this out—he was too angry. 'You don't have to thank me for everything. This is your home now too, and you're free to come and go. But…' He paused for a moment, watching her carefully. 'I will not tolerate the kind of behaviour you have displayed on your hedonistic jaunt around Europe over the last couple of years.'

Hedonistic jaunt.

Liyah had just taken a sip of her drink and she nearly choked, but she managed to swallow before she did.

She looked at her husband.

He'd seen the papers and the paparazzi photos.

The hurt that she'd felt the first time she'd realised she'd been so betrayed felt fresh again. The fact that she wasn't similarly armed with information on Sharif made her feel very defenceless now. But then she told herself she was being paranoid.

'What exactly are you talking about?'

His mouth thinned. 'The nice little portfolio my assistant put together for me, featuring your various and myriad exploits last summer in Europe, mainly on the Côte d'Azur.'

She wasn't being paranoid. Liyah's insides cramped. 'Those pictures weren't—'

He cut in. 'Weren't what they looked like? Spare me the excuses, Liyah. It was pretty clear what they were—pictures of an entitled royal socialite living to excess. But I couldn't care less what you got up to, or that you seem to like to affect this act of faux innocence and naivety. What I do care about is that you do not repeat that behaviour while you are married to me. Luckily the pictures didn't get picked up by the wider gossip sites. And we're going to keep it that way. You won't be hooking up with any of your Eurotrash party friends while you're with me.'

Liyah felt sick. She could see the pictures in her mind's eye. Lolling on the deck of a massive yacht in the sparkling Mediterranean Sea drinking champagne. Falling out of famous nightclubs being held up by so-called friends. Shopping in the most famous shops and streets of Spain, Italy, Paris... You name it, she'd been there.

Except she hadn't.

Because the girl in those pictures hadn't been her.

The words to try and explain this to Sharif trembled on her tongue, but he was like a stone. Disgusted. Disapproving. And a need to protect herself rose up. She would only be with this man for a year at the most. He didn't deserve to know the real her—the woman far removed from those pictures.

And how could she defend herself when his first impression of her had been the wanton woman he'd met at the oasis, who had shown no hesitation in jumping into bed with a complete stranger? No wonder he believed the worst.

She forced the emotion out of her voice. 'You can rest assured that I won't be a liability while we're married.'

Thomas appeared in the doorway at that moment, with perfect timing, to announce dinner.

Liyah preceded Sharif out of the room and tried not to feel like a chastened child. But it was hard when she wanted to stamp her feet and tell him that he had it all wrong. The injustice made her breathless, but she felt a stronger need not to let him see the soft, vulnerable part of her that very few had ever seen.

To Liyah's relief, Sharif hadn't brought up those lurid paparazzi shots again over their deliciously cooked dinner of tender chicken and rice infused with herbs and spices. But it appeared that he wasn't prepared to let everything go.

He leant back now, a nearly empty wine glass in his hand, and looked at her. 'I believed that someone must have hurt you, but if anything it's more likely to have been the other way around. Who was he?'

Liyah kept her face expressionless, even as she sucked in a breath at the barb. He thought she'd been acting the whole time. Feigning her reticence and lack of experience.

An image came into her head. A young man—her age. Tall, handsome. Cheeky smile. Charming. Intelligent. How easily he'd swept her off her feet and made her believe that he was truly interested in her. How easily she'd let him breach barriers she'd never allowed anyone else to, so self-protective and distrustful.

But when she'd first arrived in Europe a couple of years ago she'd been hungry to experience this new world and be a modern, independent woman. So one night she'd allowed him the ultimate intimacy.

She hadn't told him she was a virgin, too embarrassed and shy, and eager to relieve herself of the burden of innocence. But when she'd tensed at the unexpected pain on penetration he'd stopped, a horrified look on his face, clearly not expecting a fellow university student of twenty-two to still be a virgin.

For a moment she'd thought he'd force himself on her, but he'd jumped up and hurled a string of profane insults instead. And then she'd discovered that she was the butt of a random drunken bet between him and his friends to see how quickly he could get her into bed. Apparently he'd won his bet.

After that Liyah could remember covering up with tomboyish clothes. Tying her hair back. Wearing her glasses all the time. Diminishing herself as much as possible to avoid sticking out on the university campus. Drawing attention.

And yet Sharif had just had to look at her and she'd

forgotten the painful lessons she'd learnt in a heartbeat. Sheer instinct had overridden every rational bone in her body, proving that there was still a shameful hunger inside her, ready to expose her weakness for connection and intimacy at all costs. She'd learnt nothing. And this man wasn't about to believe what she had to say in her defence. So she would protect herself by playing to his low regard of her.

She pushed the hurt down and lifted her chin. 'He was nobody. I don't even remember his name.'

'I almost feel sorry for him.'

'He really doesn't need your sympathy,' Liyah forced out. Seeking desperately to get the focus off her, and ruffle Sharif's irritatingly judgemental and cool demeanour, she said, 'Considering our experience of each other, and the fact that this is a marriage in name only, will you be discreet?'

Sharif's gaze narrowed on her. Liyah's face grew hot.

He said, 'Taking lovers and causing headlines is the absolute antithesis of what I'm aiming to achieve by marrying you. I've got more important things to worry about.'

'Like what, exactly? Why is it so important to you to have a wife right now, when clearly it's not something you relish?'

Sharif looked at Liyah. Her cheeks had darkened with colour. Her eyes were flashing and he could see her chest moving up and down. She was agitated. Because he'd caught her out? Because he was setting parameters? Whatever the reason, it was having an incendiary effect on his blood and he had to shift discreetly in his seat.

He had to focus on what she'd asked. His first in-

stinct was to give her some platitude, but something
stopped him. He'd never been in this situation before,
with a woman who was ostensibly going to be by his
side for the foreseeable future. The longest liasion he'd
ever had had lasted about two weeks.

'I'm at a crucial juncture in the development of the
Marchetti Group and having a wife by my side will take
me—*us*—to the next level. That is the most important
thing, and it drives every decision I make.'

Was it his imagination or had she flinched slightly
when he'd said that? Her eyes were huge and very green.
Then she looked away and it irritated him, because usually he was the one to avoid eye contact. And why did
he feel the need to justify why the Marchetti Group was
so important when he'd never felt the need to before?

He wanted her eyes back on him. 'I've got a team
lined up to come here tomorrow and set you up.'

She looked at him again, and Sharif felt a moment of
satisfaction even as a spike of need made his body tighten.

She said, 'Set me up?'

He nodded, imagining her in a sleek satin and lace
concoction before he could stop himself. 'A stylist and a
hair and beauty team. A few others. To make sure you're
prepared for our first event on Wednesday evening.'

The colour drained out of her face slightly. 'That's
the day after tomorrow!'

Sharif nodded. 'A press release will be issued tomorrow, announcing our marriage. We've flown under the
radar so far, which is how I wanted it. But you need to
be ready to face the world I inhabit. This is going to be
far removed from the tacky haunts you frequented in
Europe and that dusty palace in Taraq.'

Her cheeks flushed again and her jaw tightened. 'It wasn't me in those—' She stopped suddenly.

'It wasn't you in what?'

She shook her head, letting her hair fall forward. 'Nothing.' Then she looked at him again and pulled at a wayward strand. 'There's not much I can do about this unless you want me to cut it off.'

To Sharif's surprise he felt a visceral rejection of that notion even as he wanted to tame it somehow, because it reminded him too much of the wildness she aroused inside him.

He shook his head. 'No need. I have the best in the business lined up—they'll make sure you're presentable.'

'Thanks.'

Sharif almost smiled at her sarcastic tone. 'Believe me, you're going to need all the armour you can get. As the wife of the Marchetti Group's CEO, your every move and item of clothing will be scrutinised with a magnifying glass. But it shouldn't be too daunting. After all, you are a princess, so you were always going to be on display to a lesser or greater extent.'

A short while later, after Sharif had excused himself to go to his study and make some calls—did the man never stop working?—Liyah was curled up in a chair in front of one of the big windows, her hands around a mug of herbal tea delivered to her by Thomas.

Manhattan looked like a magical carpet of diamonds outside. She could see the blinking lights of all the helicopters flying in the sky. Delivering more billionaires to their luxurious apartments?

Sharif's words resounded in her head. *'You were*

always going to be on display.' Was she? She knew he was right, but somehow, she'd believed that by escaping to Europe to go to university she'd somehow slip under the radar. And then Samara had needed her.

The thought of being moulded to fit into Sharif's world filled her with dread. She'd always preferred being in the background, even though she'd inevitably stood out. When she'd been a teenager she'd been gangly and uncoordinated, and then, seemingly overnight, she'd developed curves that she'd had no idea what to do with.

The women of the palace had always used to pass comment that she was too tall. Too ungainly. Not delicate and feminine like the rest of her sisters.

That had been one of the things that had attracted her to the guy who had shown her attention at university. The guy she'd trusted with her innocence when she shouldn't have. He'd been tall, although not as tall as Sharif. He'd seemed glad that she was tall, even making a joke about how nice it was not to have to bend down to kiss someone.

It had all been smooth lies to fulfil a bet.

Liyah cringed now to think of how desperate she'd been to forge a life for herself, to fit in, and how starved of attention. *Weak, for affection.*

But Sharif hadn't had to say anything. He'd just looked at her as if he wanted to devour her. She shivered now, even though the apartment was at the perfect temperature for comfort.

On an impulse, she went and retrieved her laptop from her luggage and brought it back to the living room.

Sitting cross-legged on the chair, she did what she should have done days ago. She looked up her husband.

She was immediately bombarded with a slew of paparazzi shots of Sharif with women. Lots of women. And each one absolutely stunning. Redheads. Blondes. Brunettes. All pale and sleek and elegant.

None like Liyah, with her wild untameable hair and dark skin. Something twisted painfully inside her. She clearly wasn't his type. What had happened between them at the oasis had been an anomaly. No wonder he didn't want anything more to happen.

She delved further and noted that he was rarely seen with the same woman more than a handful of times. And then she came across the recent spate of 'kiss and tells'. Women clearly unhappy with the way he'd unceremoniously ended their liaisons.

Liyah shivered again. She could imagine only too well how it must feel—like being under the scorching rays of the sun only to be suddenly thrust into the icy winds of the Arctic.

She shook her head at her fanciful imagination. It was a *good* thing to know what kind of a man he was and realise that she'd escaped relatively unscathed.

Unscathed? mocked a voice in her head. *Unscathed doesn't quite account for the fact that he's ignited a wicked hunger inside you.*

Liyah ignored the voice and purposely clicked on a link relating to the Marchetti business, moving away from incendiary images and thoughts. She read about Sharif's deceased father, who sounded like a larger than life character, bullish in his ambition to build a global brand from a handful of boutiques in Rome. He'd been a dark, masculine man. Undeniably handsome. But there was something about him that Liyah thought looked cruel.

Then she read about the speculation that he would have been nothing without the vast fortunes of each of the women he'd married. Sharif's mother was mentioned and pictured—Princess Noor, a stunningly beautiful woman. Liyah recognised her beauty in Sharif's features. The deep-set eyes. High cheekbones. Proud, regal nose.

She read about how Sharif had rebuilt the company after his father had died, having left it tainted with scandals and rumours of corruption. She read about Sharif's ruthlessness in going after legacy brands, only to strip them of everything but their name before hiring whole new teams to revitalise them.

She read about his half-brothers. Nikos and Maks. From different mothers. Both were gorgeous. Nikos was being called 'a reformed playboy', after marrying and settling down with a young family. There was a picture of him with his pregnant wife and a dark-haired baby that looked to be nearly a year old. Apparently, he hadn't known about his son until after he was born.

Maks seemed to be much more elusive. But Liyah found a picture of his recent wedding to a petite and very pretty woman with honey-blonde hair. They were coming out of a civil office in London and smiling at each other. They looked as if they were in love, and Liyah felt a flash of envy that she quickly told herself wasn't envy. It was pity—because their apparent happiness would undoubtedly be an illusion. Even staged for the cameras.

She thought of what Sharif had said about needing

to marry to take the Marchetti Group to the next level. Perhaps that was why his brothers had married too. A joint effort to stabilise the brand. That made a lot more sense to Liyah than the fanciful notion that perhaps Sharif's brothers were different from him and had married for love.

How could they possibly believe in love when they'd all come from broken marriages?

Clearly Nikos had married his ex-lover and the mother of his child only to protect the reputation of the company. What about Maks, though? And how had Sharif become the sophisticated and ruthless CEO of a vast conglomerate if he'd grown up on the other side of the world in a desert kingdom?

Liyah shut the laptop abruptly, not liking the swirl of questions in her head precipitated by the online search. She didn't need to know about Sharif or his family. She just needed to get through the next year and then she would finally be free to pursue her own goals and her own life.

She waited for a spurt of excitement and joy at that prospect, but she felt nothing except a kind of…flatness.

She scowled at herself and put it down to weariness. In spite of her nap earlier, and the nap on the plane, she was tired, and a lot had happened. It was no wonder she couldn't drum up much enthusiasm.

However, when she crept past Sharif's office door a few minutes later, and heard the deep rumble of his voice on the other side, the instant rush of adrenalin and excitement made a complete mockery of any notion that her sense of anti-climax was fatigue-related…

CHAPTER FIVE

TWO DAYS LATER, Sharif waited for Liyah to appear in the apartment's main reception room. He'd hardly seen her since that first evening—he'd been busy catching up on what he'd missed during his few days' absence.

The irony wasn't lost on him that if he was a regular person he would still be on his honeymoon. But before his brain could be flooded with tantalising images of what a honeymoon with Liyah might look like—*feel like*—he reminded himself that he wasn't a regular person, and hadn't been since the moment his father had seduced his mother with one eye on creating an heir and another on stealing her vast dowry.

Sharif put two fingers behind his bow tie and his top button in an effort to loosen them slightly. He felt constricted when he normally never did. There was a hum in his blood too—a hum of anticipation. Something he usually only associated with the prospect of bettering a rival in business or making a spectacular acquisition.

He heard a sound and instinctively tightened his fingers around the small tumbler of whisky he'd poured himself. He turned around slowly to see Liyah standing just inside the door, looking unbelievably hesitant.

And stunning.

Sharif didn't even realise his breath had stopped until his body forced him to breathe in.

His gaze followed the outline of the satin dress from the thin straps over her shoulders to the line of the bodice that cut across her chest, where the swells of her breasts were just tantalisingly visible. It went in at her slim waist and then curved out again over her hips, falling in a straight, elegant line to the floor.

It was an earthy olive-green, and it enhanced the colour of her skin exactly as he'd imagined. The design couldn't have been more simple. Deceptively simple, as he knew. He recognised haute couture as soon as he saw it. It could have been made for her, but he knew it hadn't been as there hadn't been enough time. But the material moulded to her body in a way that looked indecent enough to be bespoke.

He felt dizzy. Her hair had been straightened into a sleek fall of black silk and tucked behind her ears, where drop diamonds sparkled. But the absence of her usual unruly waves failed to diminish the incendiary memories of that night when she'd been a wild, untamed goddess, emerging from the depths of a black pool. He found this version of her more than provocative when it should be less.

He noticed that the only other jewellery she wore was a simple diamond bracelet. She held a matching green clutch bag in her hands.

She cleared her throat. 'Is it…? Am I…okay?'

Sharif was used to women fishing for compliments, and was accustomed to handing them out without even thinking, or really meaning them. Empty platitudes.

Exactly what he was expected to say. But this was un-charted territory for him.

'You are…perfect, Liyah.'

She looked away. He saw that the hands on her bag weren't quite steady.

A spike of concern made him say, 'What is it? Is something wrong?'

She moved one slim shoulder up and down. 'I guess I'm not really used to this level of attention.'

Sharif thought of those photos of her cavorting on yachts and falling out of clubs in slinky short numbers that were most definitely *not* haute couture. The spike of concern faded. Yes, she came from a royal family, but he appreciated that his world was a step up in lev-els of sophistication. Still, he had no doubt that she'd become accustomed to his world very soon.

Sharif put down his glass. 'We should go. My driver is waiting.'

He crossed the space between them and was about to take Liyah's elbow to guide her out when he stopped. Her scent filled Sharif's nostrils. A new scent. Tones of heady musky flowers conjuring up images of the hot dry desert, where exotic flowers bloomed in the most unlikely places. *Like deserted oases.*

'My ring. My wedding ring. I forgot to put it on.'

Liyah was looking up at him and Sharif realised she must be wearing heels, because her plump, lush mouth was close enough for him to see that it was slicked only with a nude sheen. Nothing as garish as red or pink lipstick.

Close up, he could see that the green of the dress made her eyes pop, and that kohl and dark shadow had turned them a light smoky green. All in all, her make-up was subtle, merely enhancing her natural beauty.

He blinked. *The ring.* 'You don't like wearing it?'

She made a face as she pulled away. 'Sorry, it's lovely—I'm just afraid I'll lose it or something.'

She turned to go back to her room—presumably to get it—and presented Sharif with a view of her smooth back. He swallowed a sound of frustration that she was getting to him like this, and forced out, 'Wait. I have something here.'

She'd distracted him enough that he'd forgotten. He'd ordered a replacement ring, because he'd seen that the other one didn't seem to fit.

She turned around and came back.

Sharif took a small box out of his inside pocket. He opened it and she looked down. He saw her inhale. It made her breasts swell against the dress. Blood surged to his groin and he clenched his jaw.

'Try it on.'

He took it out of the box and held out his hand, not even sure why he was insisting on doing it himself. Her hand was cool in his. Small. He slid the ring onto her finger. She drew her hand back and the ring sparkled, making him feel like a fraud. He cursed himself. Since when had he grown a conscience?

She looked at the ring. 'You didn't have to change it.'

Sharif put the empty box down on a nearby table. 'It's fine, I should have consulted with you in the first instance. Let's go.'

Liyah sat in the warm cocoon of the sleek car, with a couple of feet between her and Sharif. A couple of feet that she was grateful for, because she still hadn't quite recovered from seeing him waiting for her dressed in a classic black tuxedo.

The suit was clearly bespoke, showcasing the powerful lines of his body. It made him look even taller and broader than he usually did. But, while he wore the suit with the utmost elegance and propriety, Liyah wasn't fooled by the sophisticated veneer for a second.

He'd placed a voluminous fur coat over her shoulders before they'd left the apartment. She'd looked at it suspiciously, and he'd said drily, 'Don't worry—it's fake. We only work with designers who reject the harming of animals for their designs.'

She'd been grateful for the luxurious warmth when the cold Mahattan air had hit her like a slap in the face upon emerging onto the street. But after the initial shock, she'd breathed in the sharp air gratefully. It was her first time out of the apartment since she'd arrived. Till now, her only encounter with the outside world had been from her terrace, many floors above the streets, heightening the sense of unreality, which had only been compounded by the activities of the last two days.

She glanced at the new ring on her finger again. He'd surprised her, noticing that she hadn't felt comfortable with the other one. Except this one made her uncomfortable too—but for very different reasons.

It was…beautiful. And relatively discreet.

It was a diamond in a circular setting, surrounded by small baguette emeralds that extended outwards on either side. It was unusual, and something she might have actually picked for herself. But she chastised herself for thinking even for a second that he'd put any thought into it. Not when a veritable army of people had attended to every aspect of her 'look' for the last forty-eight hours.

She'd been pulled, squeezed, trimmed, measured, massaged and used as a mannequin upon which hundreds of different dresses, trouser suits, jumpsuits, casual clothes, swimwear, coats and shoes had been tried.

She'd even been consulted on what scents she preferred by a perfumier, and a signature scent had been mixed and sent to her within twenty-four hours in a beautiful crystal bottle with her name on it, embossed with gold leaf.

And underwear... Underwear so delicate and fine that it made her blush just to look at it.

The previous night Liyah had dreamt of Sharif's big hands, flicking aside wispy bits of lace from her body so he could get to her skin. She'd woken trembling and hot. Aching inside.

Liyah slid Sharif a quick furtive look. He was looking out of his window, his jaw hard. Remote. His thick hair was brushed back, curling on the collar of his coat slightly. He looked like a remote stranger. She could scarcely believe he was the same man who had led her into that tent at the oasis and fed her, before laying her down and showing her that she wasn't a freak. That she had capacity to feel such pleasure that—

'The press release has generated some interest. You should expect intense attention from the press when we arrive. Just stick close to me.'

Liyah's thoughts scattered. Sharif was looking at her and his face was cast in shadow, making the lines leaner and harsher. His eyes glittered. She gulped. No doubt he thought she was used to the paparazzi, because he believed she'd been courting their attention over the last two summers in Europe.

'Okay.'

Flashing lights in her peripheral vision made Liyah turn her head. She could see they were approaching an impressive building, with red-carpeted steps leading up to an ornate entrance. Men in tuxedoes and women in shimmering gowns were making their way into the building.

'Where is this?'

'It's the Metropolitan Museum.'

Liyah sucked in a breath. She'd heard of the famous building. Suddenly she felt very unprepared. 'What exactly is this event?'

'It's an annual gala to raise funds for a range of charities.'

The car was pulling to a stop at the bottom of the steps now. Liyah wanted to slide down to the floor of the car and avoid the masses of paparazzi lined up along each side, and the glamorous crowd. This was far removed from anything she'd ever experienced before. In terms of royalty, the Mansours were definitely country bumpkins.

But Sharif was already out of the car, leaving a blast of icy air in his wake. And then her door was opening and he was holding out a hand.

Liyah had a flashback to when he'd held his hand out to her at the oasis. This couldn't be more different…

She forced it out of her mind, took a deep breath, and let him help her from the car to join him at the bottom of the steps.

Immediately it seemed as if everyone—the guests

arriving and walking up the steps, the paparazzi, the myriad men and women in black suits with headsets, ushering the guests towards the entrance—turned as one to look at Sharif and Liyah.

Liyah was barely aware of Sharif's hand wrapping tightly around hers. Or his frowning look as he took in her face. Or his words. 'Just stay by my side.'

They started to move forward, and the crowd parted like the Red Sea to let them pass. There was a strange hush, and then all hell seemed to break loose.

'Sharif! Sharif! Let us meet your new wife!'

'Princess Aaliyah—over here!'

'Please, Princess, look over here. Who are you wearing?'

'Marchetti! Now that all of you are settling down, does this mean you're taking your eye off the ball? Losing your edge?'

Sharif stopped so abruptly that Liyah stumbled at his side. He turned to the bank of photographers to see where that last question had come from. She could feel the tension in his form.

He addressed the faceless people behind the flashing lights. 'The Marchetti Group is only getting stronger. I can assure you of that.'

And then he was tugging Liyah to his side and all but carrying her as they made their way up the rest of the steps.

As they reached the main doors, a golden glow emanated from inside a large marble foyer. More stairs led up to another level. Flaming lanterns lit their way and exotic fresh flowers scented the air. Uniformed staff expertly divested Liyah of her overcoat, so that by the time they reached the top she looked like every other woman in her glittering gown and jewels. It was opulent, and decadent, and so glamorous that she was afraid to breathe in case she made it disappear, or ruined it in some way.

Sharif held out his arm. She looked at it stupidly for a moment, before realising he wasn't holding her hand any more. She stepped forward and put her arm through his. She could feel the steely strength of his muscles against her, under his clothes. His heat. She tried to numb herself against the effect, but it was hard not to give in to the urge to cleave to his side.

And even more so when they walked into a room that was bathed in the golden light of hundreds of chandeliers. Ornate flower arrangements made up the centrepieces of round tables. People milled about chatting, networking. Soft, easy jazz came from a band near the top of the room.

They hadn't moved but a few feet forward before Sharif was stopped by someone. He introduced her to every person who approached them, and Liyah's face started to ache from forcing a smile. She gave up trying to remember names. They weren't really interested in her though—they only wanted Sharif.

He despatched all the sycophants with ruthless efficiency, indulging in no kind of small talk. Charming he was not…and yet that didn't stop people flocking to him. No, what he was, was something far more compelling…

It was somewhat comforting for Liyah to realise that she didn't feel as out of place or conspicuous as she usually did. Not with Sharif by her side. He eclipsed everything around him. Nevertheless, she wasn't unaware of the sly looks she received—mainly from other women—and the whispers as they passed by. But she held her head up and pretended not to notice.

Eventually they reached their table, which was at the top of the room, and Liyah sat down gratefully.

'Okay?'

She looked at Sharif as he spoke, taking his seat beside her. She realised she must have made a face. 'High heels aren't really my thing.'

He frowned at her, and she immediately realised that what she'd said would be at odds with the woman he thought she was. But before she could say anything else the music came to a stop and the people hushed.

Speeches were made as they were served plates of food that looked more like art installations. Liyah sipped at sparkling wine and it only added to the general feeling of unreality.

And then Sharif's name was mentioned by the MC. Liyah's ears pricked up.

'Year on year, the biggest philanthropic contribution comes from the Marchetti Group…please welcome Sharif Marchetti.'

Thunderous applause rang in Liyah's ears as she watched him get up, adjust his jacket and climb the steps to the stage. He moved with such fluid animal grace that she couldn't take her eyes off him.

Sharif's speech was brief, succinct, and surprisingly passionate. Liyah might have expected to hear cynicism in his voice, but she could tell that he actually cared about what he was saying.

After another round of rapturous applause, Sharif returned to the table. The MC wrapped up the speeches and people started to stand up and move around.

Sharif looked at Liyah, 'Ready?'

'For what?'

'To go.'

Liyah had been prepared to settle in for a long evening of boredom as Sharif batted away more sycophants, but apparently that wasn't how he rolled.

She stood up. 'Sure.' What else was she going to say?

Sharif took her hand and started to lead her through the crowd. Liyah faltered when she saw an anteroom where people were starting to dance to a popular tune. She loved dancing. She'd developed a surprising interest in, and love for clubbing when she'd been in Europe. Liking the sense of being anonymous in a crowd. Liking the music.

Sharif stopped and looked from her to the room. 'I don't dance, Liyah.'

She opened her mouth to say something—she wasn't sure what—but Sharif had already turned and begun leading her away.

They were stopped just as they reached the main door by a smirking older gentleman.

He said, 'Callaghan.'

The man inclined his head. 'Marchetti. I'd offer you congratulations, but I have to admit that the cynic in me thinks that it's a very opportune moment for you to appear with a convenient wife in tow. Your brothers and now you…allaying the jitters of the board so you're in peak position to launch—what, exactly? I haven't found out what you're up to yet, Marchetti, but I will… don't worry.'

Sharif said, 'With an imagination like that, Callaghan, you're clearly a frustrated novelist. And have you met my wife, whom you accuse of being a pawn?'

His easy, drawling tone belied the tension Liyah felt in the hand that was wrapped around hers.

The man had the grace to look sheepish as he acknowledged Liyah.

She held out her hand. 'Pleased to meet you. I'm Liyah.'

The man shook her hand perfunctorily, muttering something unintelligible, and walked off.

Sharif said something unsavoury under his breath and they walked out of the room.

'Who was that?' Liyah asked, when it became obvious that Sharif wasn't about to elaborate on the exchange.

'Him? Oh, just a freelance business reporter.'

'What did he mean about an "opportune moment"?'

'He's just looking for a story.'

Liyah wasn't convinced, but they were at the main doors leading outside now, and an attendant appeared with Liyah's coat. Sharif took it and helped her into it. Liyah couldn't help shivering when Sharif's fingers brushed the back of her bare neck when she lifted her hair out of the way.

He stilled for a moment, and then said, 'We'll be back at the apartment soon.'

He'd obviously mistaken her shiver as an indication of feeling cold. Not awareness. Thankfully. She shivered all over again under the coat at the thought of him realising just how much he affected her.

* * *

In the back of the car, Sharif heard Liyah ask, 'Do you always leave these events early? Or was it just tonight?'

He forced his jaw to unlock. It had gritted tight on the sight of that reporter. Actually, it had been gritted all evening, as he'd tried to remain unaware of Liyah beside him, sinuous and sultry in that dress—which was now, thankfully, covered up.

This was unprecedented territory for Sharif. He wasn't used to women having such a visceral pull on him. He was used to desiring women, of course, but also to relegating it very much to a place he had total control over.

He'd almost fumbled his speech because he'd been so aware of Liyah, sitting just feet away, her skin gleaming against the green of the dress. And, even more distractingly, he'd been acutely aware of the attention she'd drawn from other men. Which usually didn't bother him in the slightest, because the women he dated impacted on him only in a very peripheral way.

But Liyah is your wife, so it's natural that her effect is different.

Sharif relaxed his jaw some more. That was it.

He reached for his bow tie, loosening it. He looked at her and almost forgot what she'd asked. The soft lights in the back of the car made her seem unreadable, infinitely mysterious. All he wanted to do was clamp his hands in her hair and tug her towards him, so that he could crush that provocative mouth under his and punish her for proving to be such a distraction.

He forced his blood to cool. 'Did you want to stay

and dance? Pretend you were back in the clubs of Europe?'

'I do like dancing, actually. That's not a crime, is it?'

'Only if you end up being carried out by the bouncers.'

He watched that full mouth compress and felt his body jerk in response. He shifted in his seat.

She said, 'You didn't answer my question. Do you normally leave events early?'

Sharif instinctively chafed at the question. He didn't indulge women who wanted to know more about him. He hadn't shared his inner thoughts and motivations with anyone since his mother had died and the one person he'd trusted had gone. He kept things strictly superficial. Sexual. And then it was over. Which women did not appreciate… Hence the recent media attention, after his last lover had decided to lash out in the papers, branding him a heartless monster.

But Liyah was different. They were married. And for some reason he had a compulsion to tell her. 'I don't particularly enjoy them. And I don't see the point in hanging around when what I've needed to do is done.'

Liyah moved back into her corner of the car, as if she wanted to get a better look at him. It made Sharif's skin prickle with awareness and something else. Exposure.

'You're a bit of a lone wolf, aren't you?'

'You don't need anybody else, Sharif!'

Those words had been hurled at him too many times to count over the years. His mother had said them too, but with the emphasis on it being a good thing. She'd said, *'You don't need anybody else Sharif. Don't trust anyone. Trust yourself. You are your own best friend.*

You'll know what to do.' She'd learnt a harsh lesson at the hands of his father, when he'd betrayed her trust, stolen her inheritance and broken her heart.

So, yes, Sharif was a lone wolf. He'd become one to survive. So why was it that Liyah's observation snagged on him like a splinter piercing his skin?

'I trust myself and I ask for no one's opinion or help unless I want another perspective.'

'What about your brothers?'

A heavy weight settled in his gut. 'We didn't spend time together when we were growing up, so we're not close. But they trust me.'

As he said those words the weight got heavier. He'd never really acknowledged that before. But they did trust him. They had from the moment their father had died and he'd called them to the board and convinced them that it was in their interest to work together.

He knew that they might not admit they trusted him, and they certainly had their own reasons for wanting to work for the company their father had built up—but deep down there'd always be an affinity. Because they'd all suffered at the hands of their father.

'But you don't trust them?'

Sharif frowned sharply. Liyah was skating far too close to the truth, making guilt spike. 'I trust them as much as you trust *your* family.'

She flushed at that. He could see her skin get darker. Blood rushing to the surface. His body tightened. What was he doing…provoking her when he had no intention of slaking this lust?

'You don't know enough about me to know who I might trust.'

'Your sister? You sacrificed yourself for her.'

Sharif suddenly had an image of Liyah's pretty, but far less compelling sister. He couldn't imagine being in this situation with her and feeling this throbbing, desperate need. Which was not what he'd intended for this marriage.

'Yes, my sister. I do trust her.' She sounded defensive.

The car was pulling up to the kerb outside his apartment building now, and Sharif almost lamented the interruption. He found that he was enjoying parrying with Liyah because he didn't know what she might say next. She was unpredictable.

His door was opened by the driver and he got out and went around to open Liyah's door. She put her hand in his, the wedding ring glittering in the dark.

His insides clenched as he closed his fingers around hers. He'd never imagined putting a ring on any woman's finger. But it looked good on her. Better than the other one, which he'd only used because it was an heirloom from his mother's side of the family. He found that seeing his ring on her hand didn't make him feel as claustrophobic as he might have expected.

She stepped out, close to Sharif. For a moment he didn't move, drinking in her scent. Soft, musky. She smelled of heat and flowers.

And then suddenly she wrinkled her nose and looked up, and Sharif saw snowflakes landing on her face. Settling on her cheek.

A slow, awed smile bloomed across her face. 'It's snowing!'

Sharif found a smile tugging at his own mouth.

'That's usually what happens in New York this time of year.'

She didn't seem to hear him. She was looking up, totally transfixed. Closing her eyes and laughing softly as more flakes fell, leaving little wet trails down her cheeks.

Surprised, Sharif said, 'You've never seen snow before?'

She shook her head, making her hair ripple over her shoulders like black silk. She opened her eyes. They were a darker green in the dim light. 'Never! It feels like being kissed.'

Sharif's gaze dropped to Liyah's mouth. Soft, infinitely tempting. He was about to reach for her, put a hand under the coat to find her waist, tug her towards him so he could—

Stop. The voice sounded in his head. What was he doing, being tempted by such rudimentary tactics? She was trying to entice him.

Of course she must have seen snow before—she'd been in Europe.

But they were out on the street, with people passing. No doubt paparazzi lurking. And it was for that reason and that reason only that Sharif decided he would give in to her ruse and tug her closer, cover her mouth with his.

He heard her surprised little gasp. For a second he revelled in the feel of her yielding, melting against him, head tipping back, mouth softening. He ran his tongue along the seam of her mouth and had to stop a growl of satisfaction when she opened to him and he delved deep into her sweetness, fast forgetting why he had decided to kiss her in the first place when he knew it was a bad idea.

He sensed the change in her just before she tensed, her hands coming up between them. Sharif lifted his head. It was snowing harder now, with thick, fluffy flakes landing all around them and on Liyah's hair, face.

She blinked. 'Why did you kiss me?'

Because you couldn't not, whispered a sly voice.

In his peripheral vision Sharif saw a flash of light. 'Paparazzi. Shame to waste an opportunity to give them something to print tomorrow.'

Liar.

Sharif let Liyah push him back. She took a step to the side but then made a sudden jerking movement when her foot slipped on the icy ground.

Without even thinking, Sharif scooped her up into his arms and carried her into the apartment building, where the door was being held open by his security staff.

Liyah was still too much in shock to say or do anything as Sharif carried her into the building as if she weighed no more than a bag of sugar—when she knew she was no delicate flower.

Paparazzi.

She hadn't noticed anything. But then with Sharif standing so close and that decadent, sexy scent winding around her like invisible silken thread it was no wonder.

Delayed mortification rose inside her. She hadn't even put up a modicum of resistance. It was as if she'd been waiting for him to kiss her all evening.

They were at the elevator now, and she said stiffly, 'You can put me down now.'

At least there was the voluminous coat between them. The thought of Sharif carrying her while she was wearing just the flimsy dress was far too reminiscent of when he'd lifted her out of the bath at the oasis and carried her over to the bed.

He put her down and the doors opened. Liyah stepped in, dismayed at how shaky her legs were. Sharif got in beside her, instantly dominating the space and sucking up all the oxygen, turning it hot and making it hard to breathe. Liyah was suddenly sweltering in the coat but didn't want to take it off.

When the doors opened into the penthouse suite Liyah stepped out and finally shucked off the coat with relief. Thomas appeared as if from nowhere, and Liyah smiled her thanks as he took it and faded into the background again.

She turned to Sharif, avoiding looking at him directly. 'Please don't do that again without warning me first. I know I'm little more than an employee, but you can't just…manhandle me when it suits you.'

Liyah winced inwardly at her choice of words. It hadn't felt like manhandling. At all. It had felt delicious to be standing in the freezing cold, with snowflakes falling like feathers on her skin and Sharif's mouth on hers, incinerating her from the inside out. She could still almost feel the imprint of his hand on her waist.

He was silent for so long that Liyah risked a glance. He was smiling. *Smiling!*

He said, 'Manhandle?'

Liyah's mortification turned to anger. She crossed

her arms. 'Yes—manhandle. As in put your hands on me, and your mouth, without asking permission.'

She thought then of all the women who'd given her sly looks earlier. No doubt they wouldn't complain if Sharif *manhandled* them. In fact she was fairly certain that it was something he'd never been accused of before.

It wasn't really fair to level it at him now...but if he thought he could just kiss her like that in public with no forewarning...

Liyah went hot and cold at the same time at the thought of constantly being exposed in her desire for him.

Sharif's mouth straightened. 'Please accept my apologies. In future I will ask your permission first.'

Liyah was sorry she'd said a word now. Sharif Marchetti, also known as Sheikh Sharif Bin Noor al Nazar, was not a man who asked permission for anything. He demanded and people acquiesced. As she'd acquiesced all too easily.

Struggling to maintain a modicum of dignity, Liyah tipped up her chin. 'I'm quite tired now. I'm going to bed.'

'Goodnight, Liyah.'

She turned, and walked away as gracefully as she could, aware of Sharif's eyes boring into her back.

He was probably still laughing at her.

Sharif watched Liyah walk away, his gaze drawn helplessly to the sway of her hips. The smooth expanse of her skin above the neckline of the dress. Her bare shoulders.

She'd certainly proved to be a complementary foil

this evening. If she kept it up like that she would be the perfectly convenient wife he'd wanted.

If it wasn't for the irritating fact that you want her so badly you had to kiss her on the street like a crass boy.

Sharif ignored the inner voice and focused on the niggle of disquiet that told him a society party girl didn't change her spots so easily.

Your brother Nikos did.

He ignored that reminder too. His brother had been one of the world's most notorious playboys until he'd met his wife Maggie and then a year later had discovered he had a son. But, as Sharif liked to goad him all the time, he was sure it was only a temporary state of affairs before Nikos realised what he was missing and went back to his old ways.

After all, they were both their father's sons, and their father hadn't had a committed bone in his body. Unless you counted his commitment to fleecing his wives and using their money to build up the company...

But in the end their father hadn't even had the commitment to further his own ambitions—had become drunk and corrupt on success, wealth and status. He'd died in the arms of his latest lover, any reputation he'd built up shot to pieces. And that was when Sharif had realised the extent of his father's betrayal.

He hadn't stolen from his mother and effectively killed her for the good of anything. He had done it only to satiate his intense greed and to prove that disinheriting him had been a mistake.

Domenico Marchetti had never got over the fact that he'd been passed over in his father's will for his younger brother. Sharif's father had arrogantly assumed he'd inherit, even though he'd put no time or effort into the modest family business, but it had been left to his brother instead.

Part of Domenico's bid for power had included getting revenge on his brother by ruining the business. *His own family's inheritance.* Sharif even had a memory of his uncle—a broken man—coming to Domenico, begging for help, for mercy. Sharif's father had slapped him across the face and thrown him out on the street.

Sharif shoved aside the unwelcome rush of memories. Liyah might have been a compliant foil this evening, but she was probably just lulling him into a false sense of security before she displayed her true colours again and reverted to type.

And that would not happen. Not while she was his wife.

CHAPTER SIX

'SHE'S *WHERE*?'

Sharif stood up from the boardroom table and a dozen faces turned towards him expectantly. He waved a hand to indicate they should go on without him and walked over to one of the floor-to-ceiling windows, shoving his free hand in the pocket of his trousers.

The disembodied voice came again. 'She's in Central Park, sir…playing in the snow.'

Sharif couldn't see Central Park from where he was. It was north and he looked south, towards lower Manhattan. He cursed.

'Playing with who?'

'Er…some kids, sir.'

Sharif absorbed this.

Liyah had sent a text from the phone he'd furnished her with earlier, wanting to know if there were plans for that evening. He'd informed her that, yes, there were. They were due to attend a dinner. And then she'd asked if she could have a few hours to go out. He'd said of course she could. He wasn't her gaoler.

He'd fully expected that she would use the car to drive her from designer boutique to designer boutique.

Not that she would ditch the car and insist on walking. To Central Park. To play in the snow.

'Send me a picture,' said Sharif, then terminated the conversation with his security officer and went back to the table, sitting down again. He vaguely tuned in to the discussion, but when his phone vibrated in his pocket he took it out again.

He couldn't quite believe what he was seeing. An image of a wrapped-up Liyah, her hair reverted to its wild and unruly state since the other night, flowing from under a woollen hat around her shoulders. She was grinning at what looked like an army of small children as they launched themselves at her. In the next picture she was on the ground, covered by the same children, with snow spraying all around them.

Sharif found this utterly incomprehensible. And it was hard to compute how it made him feel. Envious? He rejected that thought. Why on earth would he be envious of—

'Sir... *Sir?*'

Sharif looked up from his phone. His chief financial advisor was looking at him with a frown.

'If we want to put these plans in motion by the end of the month, we need to sign off on this today.'

A jolt went through Sharif. What was he doing? He never let anything distract him from his endgame. And certainly not a woman.

He put his phone away—but not before sending a terse text to Liyah.

Make sure you're ready at six p.m. It's a formal dinner, cocktail dress. The styling team will meet you back at the apartment.

Sharif threw his phone down. Why did he suddenly feel like a buzz-kill?

That evening Liyah was the one waiting for Sharif to finish getting ready for dinner. Apparently he was hosting an exclusive event to welcome the new head designer of an iconic fashion house.

Liyah stood at the window, her image reflected back to her, but she wasn't seeing that.

When Sharif had arrived back, a short while ago, he'd immediately said, 'Why didn't you go shopping today?'

Liyah had been genuinely perplexed. 'Was I supposed to? I have more clothes than I could possibly wear.'

'Why did you go to the park?'

'Why not? I wanted to see the snow.'

'And those kids?'

It had been more like an interrogation than a catch-up on the day's events. But then she'd reminded herself that this was hardly a regular marriage situation. And Sharif had probably assumed she'd spend the day in a beauty salon or perhaps an opium den.

Liyah had folded her arms, glaring at Sharif, hating how even in a plain dark suit and a white shirt open at the neck he still managed to pack the same punch as if he was wearing a tuxedo.

Or nothing at all.

'They saw me in the snow. They laughed at me when I told them it was my first time seeing it. And then they started a snowball fight.'

Eventually he'd said, 'Okay.'

'Okay?' Liyah had repeated testily. 'I am allowed to go outside and play in the snow?'

His gaze had narrowed, become dark and unreadable. Liyah had noticed his unshaven jaw and deep inside a pulse had picked up pace.

'Don't provoke me, Liyah. And don't forget that you're most likely being followed by paparazzi at all times. We leave in half an hour.'

Liyah's hair and make-up had already been done, so she'd just had to put on the dress. It was snowing again outside, making Manhattan pristine.

The sight of the snow mocked her. There'd been something poignant about experiencing it for the first time on her own in the park, despite the kids. And that had freaked her out—because throughout her time away from home over the past couple of years she hadn't ever felt lonely before. And yet today she'd found her mind wandering to Sharif. Wondering what he was doing. Thinking of the way he'd moved through that room full of people last night. So alone. Tense.

He intrigued her. He seemed so different here from the man she'd met in the desert.

She moved slightly, and the reflection of the dress glittered back at her. It was a simple elegant design—A-line, tea-length, strapless. Dark bronze silk over cream tulle. She wore matching shoes and her hair had been straightened again, slicked back into a low bun at the back of her head. Kohl made her eyes seem bigger, and gold hoops in her ears swung and caught the light.

She didn't feel like herself. But she could appreciate that Sharif wouldn't want her to look as wild as she had at the oasis, or even on her wedding day—and, even though she mightn't want to admit it, this new version of herself wasn't entirely…unwelcome. In spite of her avowed tomboy tendencies, Liyah couldn't help but feel…pretty. Maybe even a little beautiful.

The sparkling green of the small emeralds in her wedding ring caught her eye. She hadn't taken it off since Sharif had put it on her finger and a prickle skated over her skin. At that moment she caught sight of him behind her, reflected in the window.

How long had he been there?

He was wearing a three-piece suit. And suddenly there didn't seem to be enough air in the room. She was glad she wasn't facing him directly, because her heart was practically jumping through her chest. It was so mortifying that he had this effect on her, when all she'd been to him was a random hook-up in a desert oasis before he had to commit to a convenient marriage.

'Ready to go?' he said from behind her.

Liyah steeled herself and turned around. 'Yes.'

She had a sudden vision of how this marriage would play out—days spent on her own interspersed with sterile social events. Playing dress-up in haute couture. She clenched her hands into fists. Why did that suddenly bother her? When the thought of her imminent freedom and independence should be enough to see her through this short period?

She moved forward, very aware of Sharif's eyes on her, coolly appraising. He held out a long camel coat and helped her into it. A classic design, it belted around her waist. She picked up her clutch bag.

In the back of the car a few minutes later, cocooned

from the bitterly cold air outside, Liyah said, 'I looked you up today.'

He turned, arched a brow.

Her face grew hot. 'I mean I looked up your company. So, you basically own all the biggest luxury designer brands and labels in the world?'

Sharif inclined his head. 'Along with the oldest and most exclusive champagne and Irish whiskey brands.'

'You have a distillery in Ireland?'

He nodded.

'Is that something you always wanted to do? Follow in your father's footsteps?'

Sharif tensed visibly, his eyes widening, and then he made a sound that was half-laugh, half-growl. 'Follow? I had no choice but to take over—or everything he'd built up would have been destroyed and all for nothing.'

Feeling her way, she said, 'You weren't close?'

She thought he wasn't going to answer, but then he said, 'Do you know when I saw snow for the first time?'

She shook her head.

'In Scotland, at a boarding school so remote you needed a boat to get to the mainland. That's where my beloved father put me after he'd had me kidnapped from my mother's home in Al-Murja.'

'Kidnapped?' Liyah was shocked. She hadn't seen anything about that in the stories she'd found online. 'Why would he kidnap you?'

'Because my mother wasn't going to just hand me over. She knew what he was like. He'd seduced her and married her just to get her dowry and set himself up. He'd humiliated her and broken her heart. She knew he only wanted me as a pawn to use in the future. Someone he could mould into doing his bidding.'

His voice was hard. Cold. Liyah couldn't push away the image of a young boy with dark hair, shivering against the forbidding backdrop of an icy country. The culture shock would have been traumatic. Especially coming from the desert. The very thought of it made her own heart ache.

'How did your mother die?'

'He killed her.' Before Liyah could respond to that, Sharif added, 'Or as good as. She got sick. She needed urgent expensive medical treatment in Europe. Her family didn't have the necessary cash—it took years for them to recover financially from the loss of her dowry, and from the humiliation of her not fulfilling the agreement to marry your uncle—and my father refused to help. When he eventually did agree to fly her to Paris for an operation it was too late. She'd died.'

'How old were you?'

'I'd just turned nine. I hadn't seen her in a year.'

A lump formed in Liyah's throat. She forced it down, sensing that Sharif was not looking for sympathy or comfort. She just said, 'That's rough.'

Sharif shrugged. 'It was what it was. It's in the past now.'

But she sensed it was not forgotten. Not by a long shot.

They were coming to a smooth stop outside a restaurant now, and Liyah could see officious-looking people springing forward with clipboards, and umbrellas to ward off the snow.

Sharif got out and opened Liyah's door. She steeled

herself against the inevitable reaction when she put her hand into his, but it was no use. By the time she got into the warm space of the restaurant her skin was hot, and she pulled away from Sharif in case he saw how weak she was.

Someone discreetly took her coat and she followed Sharif into the restaurant, gasping a little when she saw the elaborate setting. There was a long table laid with gold cutlery. An arrangement of winter flowers ran down the centre of the table in green, gold and decadent red. There were hundreds of flickering candles.

Everything became a bit of a blur as she and Sharif were swept into a round of meeting people and air-kissing before they were seated for dinner. Liyah had to stop her jaw dropping to the floor more than once when she recognised several movie stars. One of whom had won multiple awards the previous year.

To her relief, she wasn't seated beside Sharif, who was at the top of the table. The new designer and his assistant were next to him. It gave her a chance to regain her breath after the revelations he'd shared on their journey here. A chance to observe him for once. She saw how he interacted with the designer, giving him the totality of his attention, but every now and then his gaze would slide to Liyah and she'd immediately feel flustered and look away.

In a bid to avoid Sharif's eye, she got into a conversation with the woman beside her who turned out to be very pleasant. She was a stylist who regularly worked with the designer, and Liyah was able to ask her lots of questions about the fashion industry that Sharif would never have had the time to indulge.

After Sharif had given a speech, and the dinner party had started to break up, people moved into another room, from where Liyah could hear the infectious beat of disco music. Clearly the party was continuing. But when she looked around, Sharif was approaching with her coat.

'You really don't like to hang around, do you?' Liyah observed drily as he helped her into it.

'This is work for me.'

When they were back in the car, Liyah couldn't help probing. 'So, if you take a woman on a date, what do you usually do?'

Sharif didn't like the way he suddenly felt defensive. For the whole of the dinner he'd found himself distracted. Distracted by the play of golden light on Liyah's skin. The slope of her bare shoulders. Her arms, slender but strong. The graceful curve of her neck and jaw. The regal line of her profile and those ridiculously lush lips. The way she'd made everyone else look pale and listless in comparison. The way she'd listened attentively to the person beside her when everyone else in the room had been darting looks all around to see who was looking at them, or if someone more important was on the horizon.

He didn't like it that he'd noticed so much. It made him prickly on top of feeling defensive. 'Do you feel hard done by because I haven't taken you on a date, Liyah?'

Her eyes flashed. 'I know this isn't a conventional relationship. I don't expect…that.'

'That?' He mimicked her. 'You mean romance? I

don't offer women romance, Liyah—as you might have noticed from the recent salacious headlines you must have seen in your research. I offer them a very straight-forward transaction.'

'Sex.'

He shrugged unapologetically. 'In a word. I'm not interested in a relationship. Hence this...' He gestured between them to indicate their arrangement.

She was silent for a moment, and then she asked, 'Why are you so consumed by building the business if you hated your father so much?'

Revenge. Retribution. Redemption.

How did this woman get so close to his edges every time? He barely knew her, but she seemed to be able to see into a place inside him where no one else ever dared venture. Not even his brothers—and if anyone could guess at the darkness inside him it would be them.

And, worse, why did he feel the need to tell her any-thing? The story about him being kidnapped was in the public domain and yet he never spoke of it. Never spoke of that terrifying moment when a Jeep had come hurtling towards him over the sand in the desert. He'd been going to set up camp for the night on his own. At the age of eight. Because he'd wanted to prove to his mother that he could be trusted.

He'd thought at first that it was his cousins, or his uncle, but it had been white-faced strangers with scarves covering their mouths. Private mercenaries with rough hands. Too strong for him to fight.

They'd hauled him off his horse.

To this day he cursed himself for not cantering away when he'd had the chance. They'd bundled him into the

Jeep and taken him to a helicopter. And then a plane. First to Rome, where his father had laid out what was expected of him, and then to that gothic monstrosity of a school in Scotland.

He refused to visit Scotland even now.

And here was this woman, shining a light onto things he never discussed with anyone and making him aware of…what? That perhaps there was some lack in his life? Something missing?

Sexual frustration bit at his veins like the craving for a drug too long denied. He could kiss Liyah right now, give in to the carnal urge to slake his lust, and in so doing stop her looking at him as if she could see into all his hidden corners. And, more importantly, stop the irritating questions falling from those far too tempting lips.

But he knew that to give in would be to display a fatal weakness. So he said, in a tone that invited no further questions, 'I might have hated my father, but I don't allow emotions to cloud my judgement when it comes to business.'

Or when it comes to relationships, Liyah mused to herself silently as the car made its smooth progress through the streets of Manhattan.

She avoided Sharif's eye for the rest of the journey, not wanting him to see how his words had affected her, because she wasn't even sure why she felt this hollow sensation in her chest, when the fact that the man had closed his heart off long ago should have no impact on her whatsoever.

When Sharif returned to the apartment late the following night, he was uncomfortably aware that for the first time in his life he'd felt a sense of resentment at being kept at the office by work, when usually the thought of coming back to an empty apartment was unappealing. But he'd been watching the clock since late afternoon. Texting his security team to see what Liyah was doing.

She'd gone to the New York Public Library and spent hours inside.

And now, as he walked into the living area and was confronted with the sight of Liyah sitting cross-legged on a chair, in sweat pants and a soft, clingy cashmere top, with her hair piled on her head, reading a book, he knew that something wasn't adding up.

But he didn't feel inclined to worry about it right then.

He leant against the doorframe. 'I didn't know you wore glasses.'

She looked up, startled. And as he watched, her cheeks flushed darker. It had an immediate effect on his blood, bringing it to the boil after simmering all day. It was getting harder to keep his sexual frustration under control.

The glasses suited her. They made her look serious. Seriously sexy. But, as if hearing his thoughts, she took them off.

She closed the book. 'I wasn't sure what time you'd be back…if you'd have had dinner. I'm not sure how this works.'

Sharif straightened up and walked into the room. Its soft lighting gave everything a golden glow, including her. She watched him approach and desire coiled tight in his body. He undid his tie, and the buttons on his waistcoat, aware of her eyes following his movements as if she couldn't help herself.

He sat down on a chair near hers and picked up her book from where she'd put it down. A weighty tome on the history of New York.

She said, a little defensively, 'I wanted to read up about the city.'

Sharif put the book down. 'Perfectly commendable.' Although annoyingly inconsistent with the kind of person he thought she was. Right now she looked about as far removed from a partying socialite as it was possible to get.

Sharif made a mental note to get his team to make a more thorough investigation into what she'd been doing in Europe, suddenly suspicious as to why she was behaving so differently.

'Have you eaten?' he asked.

She nodded. 'Paul, the chef, made me a delicious beef stew. There's loads left over if you're hungry.'

A pang caught Sharif unexpectedly in the chest. No one had ever worried about saving him food before.

He shook his head. 'I had take-out in the office.'

Liyah made a face. 'That's not very healthy.'

Sharif smiled mockingly. 'Concerned for my welfare, Liyah? I told you—I don't need a wife, except on paper.'

Those mesmerising green eyes sparked and narrowed. 'Don't worry. I won't concern myself with your wellbeing again.'

Sharif cursed himself for goading her. Before he did something he'd regret, he stood up and put his hands in his pockets. 'You should go to bed, Liyah, it's late. And we're going to be taking a flight to Paris tomorrow night.'

* * *

Liyah was still trying to control her heart, which had been racing since she'd seen Sharif in the doorway, looking sexily dishevelled. Jaw stubbled. He loomed over her now, and she scrambled up from the chair and moved to the window, putting some distance between them.

Whenever he was around it felt hard to breathe.

She felt prickly—because she'd been unprepared to see him again, even after a day apart. *Not* prickly because she'd felt a little abandoned. She didn't like the sensation that she was in control of so little. Not helped by Sharif's effect on her.

'I have no objection to going to Paris, but a bit of forewarning would be nice.'

A muscle in Sharif's jaw pulsed. But he said equably, 'I'll arrange for my assistant to forward you my schedule, so you know what's coming up.'

'Thank you.' Now she felt as if she was overreacting.

Sharif shrugged minutely. 'No problem. I should have thought of it before now.'

'What's happening in Paris?'

'Some meetings with my brother and our team there, and there's an event to attend.'

'What kind of event?'

'A charity ball.' Sharif glanced at his watch. 'I have some more work to do this evening. The stylist will come tomorrow to make sure you have all you need for the trip.'

Liyah felt a spurt of relief that she wouldn't have to figure it out herself, but at the same time she felt indignation that he didn't trust her to pack the right things.

He turned and left the room, and Liyah's eyes were drawn helplessly to his fluid grace. All that taut energy. She turned around, disgusted with herself, and then groaned when she saw her reflection in the darkened window.

She imagined how Sharif had seen her just now. Hair piled up. Leisurewear. No make-up. Wearing glasses, reading a book. It was no wonder he didn't desire her any more. And that was fine with her.

Just fine.

Paris

'You like to be high up, don't you?'

Liyah couldn't keep the amused tone from her voice as she looked around Sharif's Paris apartment. It was on the top floor of a stunning nineteenth-century building, with views from almost every window of the Eiffel Tower in the near distance. It had a terrace and an elegantly modern interior design.

'I appreciate a good view.'

Liyah turned around to face him. 'Yes, but how often do you actually look at it?'

'Has anyone ever told you that you ask a lot of questions?'

Liyah blanched as a nanny's voice came back into her head. *'Always with the questions, Aaliyah. No one wants a princess who asks too many questions for a wife.'*

She'd been about six, and even at that young age she'd decided that if she couldn't ask questions then she didn't want to be a princess, or anyone's wife.

'What is it?' Sharif's voice was sharp.

Liyah shook her head. 'Nothing—just a moment of déja-vu.'

He looked at his watch. 'I'm afraid I have to go straight to the office, but I'll take you to lunch in a few hours. You should get some rest.'

Liyah had slept on the plane—an overnight flight, bringing them into Paris early in the morning. She'd noticed that Sharif hadn't slept. He'd been on his laptop or his phone the whole time. He evidently didn't need sleep, like mere mortals.

'I'm okay. Actually, I might take a walk around... stretch my legs.'

Sharif shrugged. 'Whatever you want. One of the security team will go with you.'

Liyah opened her mouth to object, but shut it again when she saw the look on Sharif's face. It wasn't worth arguing. Even though she came from a royal family, they'd never been important or rich enough to merit serious protection. But she was at another level now.

He left the apartment, and after Liyah had freshened up she explored a little more, finding a media room and a gym with a lap pool. It looked very inviting, but she wanted to get out into the fresh air and see Paris again. It was one of her favourite cities.

She bundled up against the cool late winter breeze and set out to the Eiffel Tower, which was further away than she'd thought. An optical illusion.

When she reached it, she stood in the plaza among lots of other tourists milling around, and looked up at the majestic structure. Paris had been the first foreign city she'd visited after London, and she'd adored wandering around, getting lost in the *arrondissements*, sitting in cafés and lingering over coffee, watching the world go by.

You were lonely, though.

Liyah pushed the voice aside. *Not* lonely. Independent. Happy.

She saw her security man a few feet away, on his phone, his face towards her, his eyes hidden behind black shades.

Liyah went over. 'Is that Sharif?'

The man hesitated before nodding.

Liyah held out her hand, and he gave her the phone with clear reluctance. She said into it, 'Hello, Sharif.'

There was silence at the other end, and then a sigh. 'Yes, Liyah?'

'If you're so concerned about where I am and what I'm up to you should leave your stuffy meeting and come and see some sights for yourself.'

He had said he would meet her for lunch, but she didn't believe that. Anyway, she was used to occupying herself.

But then Sharif said, 'I'll meet you there. Wait for me.'

He terminated the call and Liyah handed back the phone, a little stunned. And excited. She turned away from the security guard, who pocketed his phone again and resumed his stony-faced position. Liyah tried but failed to block out the fluttery feeling in her belly.

Sharif saw her before she saw him. She was sitting on a low wall facing the Eiffel Tower. She was wearing jeans, Chelsea boots, and a dark green turtleneck under a leather bomber jacket with a sheepskin lining. Her hair was pulled up into a bun, with curling wayward strands framing her face. She also wore sunglasses. No different to many of the monied tourists around her, but a world apart at the same time.

She was drawing attention just sitting still. Her natural beauty too obvious to ignore. But she appeared not to notice. Before, Sharif would have immediately been cynical about that, believing that she was well aware of the attention she attracted. But now…he couldn't be sure.

He'd been right to investigate her more thoroughly. The fact that she'd flipped the tables on him *again* was becoming irritating in the extreme.

CHAPTER SEVEN

'How did you get a table here at such short notice?' Liyah asked, taking in the astounding views all around them from the ultra-exclusive restaurant in the Eiffel Tower. Then she rolled her eyes and answered herself. 'Stupid question, don't bother answering.'

She looked at Sharif, who was still in the three-piece suit that he'd changed into on the plane before landing. He looked as fresh as if he'd just woken from a ten-hour sleep.

The waiter came and took their orders. Even though they weren't near the top, they were still high enough that people looked like ants down below, milling around at the bottom of the tower.

Liyah said, 'I was only joking when I said that you should come. I didn't mean to break up your day.'

'I said I'd meet you for lunch.'

The waiter returned with white wine and poured two glasses. Sharif lifted his and said, *'Santé.'*

Liyah clinked her glass with his. *'Santé.'*

She took a sip, but was very aware of Sharif's gaze, which had turned calculating. She suddenly felt nervous and had no idea why.

He said nothing at first. Over a delicious starter of asparagus, and a main course of chicken breast, he lulled Liyah into a false sense of security by conducting a light conversation regarding her likes and dislikes—everything from movies to books and art.

Apparently he too enjoyed twisty dark thrillers, and he revealed a surprisingly nerdy interest in comic books.

He said, 'There were tons of them in my Scottish boarding school. I used to take piles of them and hide in one of the gardener's sheds, and get lost in them for hours. It was worth the punishment when the staff thought I'd run away.'

Liyah gasped. 'They punished you?'

Sharif's mouth flattened. 'It wasn't a good place.'

He put down his glass of wine and leant forward.

Liyah was still thinking of that dark-haired young boy, being subjected to some awful humiliation, far from home, griefstruck, so when Sharif asked, almost idly, 'When were you going to tell me that it isn't you in those paparazzi shots?' Liyah almost missed it.

Her skin went clammy. Maybe she'd heard wrong. She'd been distracted. 'What did you say?'

'You heard me. It wasn't you in those paparazzi pictures.'

'How do you know?'

'Because I looked at them properly after I realised you weren't behaving like a spoiled socialite. Far from it.'

Liyah felt as if a layer of her skin had been stripped back. Incredibly vulnerable.

Sharif sat back. 'What I want to know is why you

wouldn't tell me the truth when I confronted you about it? Why pretend to be something you're not?'

Liyah admitted defeat. 'The day you brought it up... it seemed easier just to let you believe what you wanted. I barely knew you. Everything had happened so fast.' She avoided his eye and plucked at her napkin. 'I guess it felt like a kind of armour. I wasn't ready to let you know who I was, and you didn't seem inclined to want to know.' She looked at him. 'You were too busy telling me that I was pretty much a bought companion, purely for public appearances.'

Sharif had the grace to look slightly discomfited. 'Yes, well... I was still coming to terms with the fact that *you*, the mystery woman from the oasis, and my new wife were one and the same. And you have to admit that your behaviour that night—*our* behaviour,' he amended, 'didn't exactly dissuade me from believing the worst.'

'That was part of it too,' Liyah admitted. 'I didn't think you'd believe me.'

'So, if you weren't tripping on and off yachts and spending up a storm and falling out of nightclubs, what *were* you doing?'

Sharif's gaze was direct and unwavering. Liyah tipped up her chin. 'I do like to dance, and I did go to nightclubs.'

'But, like most people, you probably managed not to fall out of them. Who's the girl in the pictures?'

'She's a Middle Eastern model. One of my sisters spotted that she looked like me. Same hair. Height...'

'She's totally different. She's about half your weight and she has no breasts.'

He glanced at her chest, making Liyah all too conscious of her larger than fashionable breasts under the soft fabric of her sweater. And her nipples were reacting to his look right now, growing hard, tingling…

She said in a strangled voice, 'I think we look totally different too, but she worked for what my father wanted and so he paid her to behave like a spoiled socialite and then tipped the press off that it was me.'

Sharif—thankfully—lifted his gaze back up to Liyah's face. 'Why would he do that?'

Liyah tried to ignore the familiar pang of hurt. 'Because telling people I was misbehaving all around Europe was preferable to admitting that I had left Taraq to try and live an independent life, which is all I've ever wanted.'

'What were you doing?'

Liyah's heart was beating fast. She hated it that it mattered to her what Sharif thought. 'I got a place at Oxford. I did a Master's in Economic and Social History over two years.'

'A Master's? Had you done an undergraduate course?'

Liyah shook her head. 'No, I'd studied for the Baccalaureate with a tutor in Taraq, and I did an interview, and they accepted me.' Liyah's mouth twisted. 'I'm sure being an international student with ready funds helped.'

Sharif shook his head. 'They're more discerning than that at Oxford. How many languages do you speak?'

'Arabic—obviously. English, French, and passable Italian and Spanish.'

'And if you were here for the summer holidays, and not falling out of clubs and onto yachts, what were you doing?'

'One summer I worked in a vineyard in France, picking grapes, and I also worked in the library at Oxford.'

'And your family were *angry* that you were doing that?'

'My father is conservative. He doesn't approve of my desire for independence. To be honest, I didn't expect them even to notice that I was gone.'

Liyah looked directly at Sharif, daring him to pity her. This wasn't about self-pity—even if her family's disregard for her had brought pain.

'My father turned his back on me a long time ago—after my mother died. He moved on with his other wives and children.'

Sharif said tautly, 'That's why I have no intention of having children. I've only known a father to be a destructive force, and I wouldn't wish that on anyone else.'

Before, Liyah would have agreed with Sharif, but something rogue made her say now, 'We're not our fathers.'

'Do you want children?'

In all honesty, Liyah wasn't sure any more. 'I want a life of freedom and independence. I don't see how children fit into that. And I'm aware that's selfish.'

Sharif shook his head. 'It's not selfish to want what most people take for granted. You'll have all the freedom you want within a year at the latest, Liyah. You'll be wealthy enough to do whatever you want, wherever you want.'

Once again, instead of relief, Sharif's words precipitated an ominous ache inside her. It was the same hollow sensation she'd felt when he'd laid out so succinctly that he didn't want a relationship...

There was a low beeping sound and Sharif picked up his phone, which had been face-down on the table. Liyah blinked and looked around. She'd been so caught in the bubble of Sharif's focus that she hadn't noticed that the restaurant had emptied around them.

He was speaking into his phone now. 'Okay, we'll see you there.' He put his phone away and said, 'That was my brother Nikos. He and his wife Maggie will also be at the charity ball tonight, so you'll get to meet them.'

'They live in Paris?'

Sharif nodded as he gestured to one of the staff for the bill. 'They also have a house in Ireland, and they spend a lot of time there. Maggie's Scottish, but was brought up in Ireland. They have a son, Daniel, who is about eight months old, and Maggie is pregnant with their second child.'

Liyah squinted at Sharif. 'So, you have a nephew and another one, or a niece, on the way?'

Sharif made a face. 'It's a girl, apparently. And my other brother Maks has just announced that his wife is pregnant too.' He stood up. 'I'm afraid I have to go back to the office, but my driver can take you to the apartment. We'll leave for the ball at seven p.m.'

Liyah stood up too, still absorbing the fact that Sharif's brothers seemed to be well on their way to creating families. Surely if they had only got married for appearances' sake, like her and Sharif, they wouldn't be actively having babies?

As they walked back outside Sharif put on his overcoat and sunglasses. Liyah saw the women nearby—and the men—doing double takes. And then third takes. She rolled her eyes.

Sharif said again, 'Take my car.'

Liyah said, 'It's okay. I'll walk back to the apartment.'

'Suit yourself. A stylist will bring some dresses by for you to choose from. It's a black tie event.'

Liyah was turning away when Sharif called her name. She stopped. He came and stood in front of her. She couldn't see his eyes behind the dark shades.

He said, 'Don't let them touch your hair. Leave it loose.'

Liyah's heart hitched. 'Why? It's so messy—'

'Just…don't touch it.'

He turned and walked away, long strides putting distance between them within seconds. Liyah looked after him, afraid of the very tender sensation she could feel near her heart because he wanted her to look like…*her*. Especially after what she had just revealed—the truth about her European trip. The truth of who she was.

A bit of an academic nerd. Someone who wanted to travel. And read. And be independent. Someone most of her family didn't really care about.

The fact that Sharif had realised himself that she wasn't the girl in the photos had hit Liyah in a very deep and secret place, where she hid her hurts and vulnerabilities. It was all too seductive to read a deeper meaning into Sharif's comment about leaving her hair in its natural unstyled state.

But then Liyah castigated herself and turned abruptly and walked away in the opposite direction. She was being ridiculous. There was no deep or hidden meaning in Sharif wanting her to leave her hair alone. Absolutely none. No matter how much she might want there to be.

And *that* was something that she definitely was not going to acknowledge.

That evening, Liyah took a deep breath as she stood in front of the mirror. It was crazy—she knew she was a princess—but increasingly she actually *felt* like a princess.

The dress was strapless, with a sweetheart neckline and low back. How it stayed up was a feat of engineering and bodice work that Liyah didn't understand, but it felt secure. It was in the most delicate shade of blush pink, almost nude with a golden embroidered overlay. It had a cinched-in waist and a full, long tulle skirt and a small train that made it dramatic without being too loud.

The dress shimmered and glistened when she moved, and with it she wore gold hued high heels.

A very nice girl had appeared with the stylist, to do her hair and make-up, and the stylist had brought her pink diamond earrings and a matching bracelet.

The women had left not long ago, and now Liyah looked at herself again. Her hair was down, as requested, and the girl had brushed it until it flowed like ripples of silk over her shoulders, the unruliness tamed somewhat.

There was a knock on the door. Liyah's heart slammed against her breastbone. She opened it, and her eyes widened as she took in Sharif in a white tuxedo jacket, with a white shirt and black bow tie. He looked dark and sexy.

There was silence. And then Sharif said, 'You look…
stunning, Liyah.'

She felt shy. 'Thank you. So do you.'

They went down to the foyer of the building, where
the concierge held open the door and their driver was
waiting, helping Liyah into one side of the car while
Sharif got into the other.

The dress had a thigh-high slit and Liyah held
the edges together over her thigh for the duration of
the journey. Not that Sharif would even notice if she
stripped naked, she was sure.

When they arrived at a seriously opulent-looking
hotel, Sharif got out and came around, opening her door.
He helped her out and kept hold of her hand, leading
her onto the red carpet.

They stopped for the ubiquitous pictures. Liyah tried
not to flinch every time a flash went off, wondering if
she'd ever get used to it.

Beside her, Sharif said, *sotto voce*, 'That was one of
the first things to make me suspect that perhaps there
was more to you than you'd told me.'

'What was that?'

'Your lack of ease in front of the photographers. I
noticed it at the Met.'

She looked up and met his gaze. A moment passed
between them—a sense of affinity, delicate and ephem-
eral. His eyes moved to her mouth and he lifted a brow
in question. Liyah knew what he was asking and she
gave one tiny nod, her skin prickling all over in anticipation.

His head descended and his mouth brushed hers,
light enough to tease, but strong enough to make her

move closer, making a small sound. Her free hand went to his chest and he caught it there.

Then he pulled back. The world was a deafening clatter of sound and flashing lights.

'Mr Marchetti, another kiss, please!'

'Princess Aaliyah—over here. Who are you wearing?'

Liyah felt dizzy, but she watched as Sharif calmly faced the photographers and said, 'Mrs Marchetti is wearing Elie Saab couture.'

He moved forward and Liyah followed unsteadily, trying to get her hammering heart back into a normal rhythm. He'd barely kissed her, and it had been purely for the cameras, but she was reduced to jelly. What would happen if he kissed her in private?

Not going to happen, she reminded herself.

By the time they reached the main reception she was marginally under control again.

Sharif stopped suddenly and said something in Italian that she didn't catch. Then he turned to her, pulling his phone out. 'There was something I wanted to show you before we left the apartment, but I got distracted.'

Liyah's heart sped up again. Had she distracted him? She hoped so, because he distracted *her* all the time.

He handed her his phone. It was a press release, headed with the Marchetti Group's logo.

We accept the apology from Celebrity! Magazine, which published photos of a woman last year, claiming them to be of Princess Aaliyah Binte Rashad Mansour.

It was, in fact, a model called Ameera Sayam. Celebrity! Magazine have agreed to donate an

*undisclosed amount of money to a charity chosen by
the Marchetti Group, and extend their apologies for
having caused Mrs Aaliyah Marchetti any distress.*

The words swam ominously in front of Liyah's eyes
and she quickly blinked. Until that moment she hadn't
realised how hurtful it was that her own father had betrayed her in such a way. And now Sharif had gone out
of his way to clear her name.

She handed back his phone. 'Thank you…you didn't
have to do that.' Her voice was husky.

'I did, actually. Your reputation now affects me and
the Marchetti Group.'

Liyah's emotions shrivelled. He'd done it for prag-
matic reasons. Not for *her.* 'Of course.'

A waiter approached and Sharif took two glasses of
champagne, handing Liyah one. She avoided his eye and
took a quick sip, hoping he wouldn't notice anything.
What was it about this man? She'd been more aware of
her emotions in the past couple of weeks than she had
her whole life.

And of your desires, pointed out a wicked inner
voice.

Sharif took her hand again and led her into the
crowd. She'd never seen so many beautiful people in
her life. Women in shimmering dresses like hers. Bling-
ing with jewels… The smell of perfume was almost
overwhelming…

And then from behind them Liyah heard a voice.

'There they are! Sharif!'

Sharif turned around and Liyah followed him to see
a man approaching. He was as tall as Sharif and very

dark, with thick curly hair. He was also astonishingly good-looking, with a classical beauty that reminded Liyah of a Greek statue. She recognised Nikos from the pictures she'd seen on the internet.

And the woman beside him. Tall—as tall as Liyah, if not taller—and very pale, with golden russet hair piled high, huge blue eyes.

She looked at Liyah and exclaimed, 'You must be Aaliyah!' She stuck out a hand. 'I'm Maggie. It's so nice to meet you.'

Liyah instinctively relaxed. Maggie was so friendly and open that it was impossible not to smile.

She shook her hand. 'It's Liyah, please—only my father calls me Aaliyah, and that's not a good thing.'

Maggie shook her hand and widened her eyes even more. She leant forward and whispered, 'Say no more. I understand all about Daddy issues. And as for these two…' Maggie gestured with her head towards Sharif and Nikos, who were watching them.

Liyah stifled a giggle. Nikos was rolling his eyes, but a smile played around his mouth as he wrapped an arm around Maggie's waist and pulled her to his side, whispering something in her ear that made her blush. It was then that Liyah noticed the bump under the form-fitting silk of her beautiful black evening dress.

'Congratulations,' she said.

Maggie put a hand on her neat bump and made a face. 'Thanks. It won't be easy, having two under two, but I like the idea of Daniel having a sibling close to his own age. I was an only child, and I always wanted brothers and sisters.'

Liyah was tempted to mention the fact that having a lot of siblings didn't exactly spell happy families...

'Liyah, this is Nikos.'

Sharif was introducing her to his brother. Liyah shook his hand, shyer than she'd been with Maggie. Nikos was smiling, and she could see how charming he was, but she could also detect that Marchetti steeliness.

These two were so clearly in love that Liyah felt bad for having entertained cynical doubts. She was very aware of the chasm between her and Sharif. Which was crazy, because love had no place for them.

Maggie was easy to talk to, and refreshingly normal in a world that Liyah barely recognised any more. She noticed that Sharif was tense around Nikos, but also how he couldn't help smiling at whatever Nikos said. She sensed that Sharif wanted to let his guard down, but wouldn't. Or couldn't.

They gradually moved closer to a central ballroom, where waltz music was playing. Maggie nudged her husband. 'You should ask Liyah to dance, Nikos—after all, we never got to celebrate the wedding.' She sent a look to Sharif, who just arched a brow.

Liyah was embarrassed, but before she knew how to respond Nikos was bowing before her and saying, 'If you would do me the honour, I'd love to have this dance.'

Relieved by the distraction, and wondering how much these two knew about the reality of her marriage with Sharif, Liyah put her hand in her brother-in-law's and let him lead her onto the dance floor. It was some-thing of a respite to spend time with a man who didn't affect her so acutely. Who didn't look at her and make her skin feel tight and hot.

Nikos was a good dancer, fluid and strong. And she breathed out and let him take control.

He said above her head, 'That bad, eh...?'

She looked up. 'Excuse me?'

He winked. 'I heard that sigh of relief. And I know how tough it is spending time with Sharif, so I don't envy you.'

Immediately Liyah felt defensive. 'He's really not that bad.'

At all.

Nikos looked at her and she blushed. 'You...you do know? That the marriage isn't...'

'All I know,' he said diplomatically, 'is that I think you'll be good for him. He works too hard and he's too serious. I'd imagine that any adjustment in his life to accomodate someone else is a good thing.'

'He's told me you didn't grow up together?'

Nikos made a face. 'No, our beloved father didn't approve of us half-brothers actually getting to know one another. He had plans for us all in the business, and was counting on us competing against one another to keep the Marchetti Group on its toes. The fact that he wouldn't approve of us working together is something that makes things even sweeter now. Sharif was the one who pointed out to Maks and I that it was *our* legacy to protect.' Nikos shook his head 'But after what happened to him and his mother, I don't know how he didn't destroy it all at the first opportunity.'

'You wouldn't have minded?'

Nikos grimaced. 'I didn't care about much until I met

Maggie again and knew I had a son. Now everything is changed.' He looked at Liyah and smiled. 'I blame my wife for the fact that I can't seem to keep anything to myself these days.'

Liyah smiled too. 'She's very sweet.'

Nikos looked over her head, presumably at his wife, and said, 'Yes she is.' And then, in an ominous voice, 'Incoming—behind you. I warn you now: the man is a terrible dancer.'

Nikos disappeared into the crowd just as Sharif appeared in her eyeline. He was glowering after his brother. They stood in the middle of the dance floor, with couples moving around them.

Sharif took Liyah's hand and moved to walk off, but she dug her heels in and hissed, 'It's the middle of the song.'

Sharif faced her. 'I told you I don't do this sort of thing.'

Liyah stepped close to him. Lifted her hands. For a moment Sharif looked so like a petulant little boy that she had to bite back a laugh. But then he muttered something and took her into his arms.

Instantly flames raced along Liyah's veins. Her core grew heavy and hot with desire. Sharif didn't have his brother's fluidity, it was true, but he moved with competent grace for such a big man.

Liyah looked up. 'Why do you hate dancing so much? You're not as bad as—' She cut herself off at Sharif's sharp look.

'Nikos oversharing again? Marriage and fatherhood have turned his brain soft.'

When he didn't say anything else, Liyah prompted, 'Well…?'

Sharif sighed. 'My father made me go to the Bal des Débutantes, here in Paris.'

'I know of it… I didn't go, but my sisters did.'

Liyah felt the familiar prickle of shame and tried to ignore it. The Bal des Débutantes was an invitation-only exclusive event, designed to introduce prominent young men and women of the world to society. Obviously she hadn't been deemed prominent enough by her family.

Sharif said, 'You were lucky. My father and I were both invited. Except my father didn't turn up. I missed the waltz class before the event and I was the only *cavalier* at the ball who didn't know how to dance. Throw in the fact that my father was reaching nuclear levels of press coverage at the time, and my mixed race heritage among the blue-eyed Princes of Europe made me stand out like a sore thumb… It didn't end well.'

Liyah's eyes widened. 'You got into a scrap?'

Sharif lifted the hand holding hers and pointed at a scar by his jaw.

Liyah reached out and ran her finger along the small indentation.

The moment Liyah's finger touched Sharif's skin an electric jolt went right down to his solar plexus. He stopped moving. She looked up at him, eyes huge. Her hair flowed over her shoulders, marking her out amongst all the other women with their complicated up-dos and overdone faces.

He didn't know what had compelled him to tell her to leave her hair down.

Yes, you do. You wanted to see her again as you saw her that night. Naked. Wild.

He shoved the provocative thought aside.

Once again she made everyone else pale in comparison. She was vibrant. Full of an earthy sensuality that called to him on such an urgent and deep level that Sharif knew he was fighting a losing battle.

She barely had to touch him and he burned. He felt volatile, and it hadn't been helped by seeing Nikos and Maggie.

Being around his brothers, and now their wives, always put him on edge, left him filled with mixed emotions. Protectiveness, regret, affection... But also a strong instinct not to trust—and guilt. Because he hadn't told them everything he was planning.

Just seeing Liyah dancing with Nikos, smiling at whatever he was saying, had made the darkness inside him lash and roar, even when he knew for a fact that Nikos had eyes only for Maggie. He'd learnt not to test Nikos's loyalty in that regard, and now, with Maggie pregnant again, they inhabited a place that Sharif could not understand.

Seeing them so happy brought back painful echoes of his relationship with his mother. Her unconditional love and his feeling of security. Something that he'd told himself he would never need again, because the pain of losing it had been so great.

Sharif gritted his jaw. He really wasn't in the mood for these introspective thoughts. And yet here was Liyah, her huge green eyes looking up at him and making him feel as if she was seeing all the way down to where he kept his darkness hidden.

He'd noticed the emotion in her eyes when he'd shown her the press release about those paparazzi photos claiming to be of her. He knew damn well that he could have left it alone…that his comment about her reputation hadn't been entirely true—those photos had barely made a dent in the mainstream gossip columns. But he'd seen how much it had affected her when she'd told him about it, and he'd wanted to avenge her. So he'd instructed his legal team to extract an apology and a retraction from the magazine or force them to face a lawsuit.

They'd issued the press release within hours.

Sharif was aware of the song coming to an end and the sense of exposure mixed with those other volatile emotions in his gut boiled over. He needed to shut out the voices and the swirling thoughts and refocus. And he knew only one way to do that.

Stop denying himself. Stop denying them both.

He led Liyah off the dance floor, his blood pounding. They were almost at the main entrance when he felt her pulling on his hand. He stopped, looked at her.

She said, 'I know you don't like to hang around, but we literally just got here.'

Sharif felt drunk with lust. The light made her skin gleam dark golden. The swells of her breasts above her bodice were a provocation he had no intention of resisting any longer. He'd forgotten why he'd ever thought it would be a good idea *not* to sleep with his wife.

He felt it in her too. She trembled whenever he touched her. Even now a blush was rising into her cheeks, staining them darker.

She said, 'Why are you looking at me like that?'

'I don't think this is working.'

ABBY GREEN 147

She frowned. 'You don't think what isn't working?'

But Sharif was striding through the lobby of the hotel now, cutting a swathe through the throng of guests, Liyah's hand clamped firmly in his.

Liyah said from behind him, 'What about Nikos and Maggie? Don't we need to say goodbye? Don't you have people to meet?'

'Nikos can look after it. I'll send him a text.'

They walked outside and a valet scrambled to call Sharif's car and driver around. He felt Liyah shiver beside him and took off his jacket then put it on her.

He texted Nikos.

We've left. Will you cover for me?

He got a text back almost straight away.

Of course. Welcome to my world, brother.

There was a winking emoji, and then a laughing crying emoji.

Sharif scowled and shoved his phone back in his pocket. This, with Liyah, was nothing like what Nikos had gone through with Maggie. For a start, she'd had Nikos's son—when he'd met her again, he'd been a father.

Sharif felt desperate. Almost feral. Things he never usually allowed himself to feel. He was always so careful to show the world that he was not his wayward father. Or his playboy brother. But he didn't have a playboy brother any more. Right now he was channelling the Marchetti rebelliousness all by himself and he couldn't care less.

He wanted his wife.

CHAPTER EIGHT

LIYAH ABSORBED THE heat and scent from Sharif's jacket as the car pulled to a smooth stop beside them. He opened the door and she got in. She didn't know what was going on with him, but she desperately resisted the temptation to believe that the heated look in his eyes meant something.

They joined the crazy Paris traffic and Liyah said nothing at first. Waiting to see if Sharif would elaborate. But he was silent. Brooding.

Eventually Liyah had to break the growing tension. 'Um…what you said about something not working… what did you mean?'

Sharif turned to look at her, snapping out of his brooding mood. He lounged back against the side of the car. Liyah had never seen him like this. It intimidated her as much as it excited her. There was something careless about him. No… Something reckless. Dangerous.

'I meant that I don't think our current arrangement is working.'

The driver put up the privacy shield between the front and the back seats.

Liyah's stomach plummeted. She'd asked too many

questions. She didn't fit into his world. She didn't look like those other effortlessly soignée women. He didn't want to dance. Not with her, anyway.

And why was her first reaction dismay?

Terrified he'd see how much he'd got to her, Liyah said stiffly, 'I think you're right. Obviously neither of us are really suited to this…arrangement—'

'I don't mean that—' Sharif interrupted her, but then broke off abruptly. He cursed.

Liyah realised the car had stopped moving, they were back at his apartment.

Before she could try to figure out what he *had* meant he was out of the car, opening her door and reaching for her, taking her hand and leading her into the building. When they were in the elevator he didn't let go of her hand. Still he didn't say anything.

Electricity crackled in the air between them. She was afraid to look at him, or put a name to it, or think about what it meant. But she could feel it in her gut. Desire. The flames were getting loose and licking at her insides. But what if she was wrong? What if—?

The elevator doors opened and Sharif led her into the apartment's foyer. The door closed behind her and Sharif let her hand go. She wobbled a little in her heels. Why was she out of breath all of a sudden?

Feeling incredibly nervous, she started to babble. 'I liked Nikos and Maggie. They're genuinely in love, aren't they?'

Sharif's expression was stark. He looked at her as if he'd never seen her before and then he said, 'I don't know much about love—but I know about *this*.'

Liyah frowned. 'About—?'

But her words were cut off when Sharif clamped his hands on her waist and pulled her into his body. All the air left her chest.

'This marriage in name only is not working.'

The look in his eye was explicit. His body was hard. His heart hammered under her hands, which were splayed across his chest. Liyah opened her mouth and then shut it again. The flames of desire licked higher. But even as they did, and as she became aware of the full meaning behind Sharif's declaration, she felt the need to resist.

'Are you sure that's a good idea?'

'I want my wife.' He growled the words.

It took a second for her to absorb that fact. To acknowledge how badly she'd wanted him to want her. How much it had flayed her inside to think that one night had been enough for him.

Then it sank in. Stark. Unvarnished.

I want my wife.

This was how he did it. No romance. He hadn't even said *I want you.* She was a commodity to him. He just wanted to scratch an itch—she was no different from his other lovers. Maybe seeing his brother with his wife had made him realise that he was missing convenient sex in his convenient marriage.

That suspicion made something close down inside Liyah.

She took a step back, dislodging Sharif's hands. 'Well, I don't think I'm prepared to renegotiate the parameters of this arrangement just because you want someone to warm your bed. I'm sure you have plenty of contacts you can call to alleviate your...urges.'

Deep inside, Liyah wondered what on earth she was saying. She was willingly pushing him into another woman's bed! But he'd never been hers in the first place. Not really. No matter how serendipitous or magical that night at the oasis had felt.

'I told you—I don't need any adverse press at this time.' He took a step towards her.

Panic at his proximity and her own weakness made Liyah put out a hand as if to ward him off. *Or grab him and bring him closer?* teased a sly inner voice.

She dropped her hand. 'So now I'm convenient not just for a marriage but also to scratch a physical itch?'

He took another step closer. His scent wrapped around her like a siren call. Woody and oriental. Infinitely seductive. She wanted to close her eyes, breathe him in until she was dizzy.

He made a sound like a strangled laugh. 'Believe me, there's nothing "convenient" about how you make me feel.'

Panic spiked. 'I don't mind if you want to take someone else to bed. I won't say anything.'

He came closer, as if she hadn't spoken. Liyah felt as if she was under water. His hands were opening his jacket that was still on her and pushing it apart, over her shoulders and down her arms. It fell to the floor at her feet with a muted swish of fabric.

He said, almost to himself, 'The problem is that I don't want anyone else. I only want you.'

You. Not *my wife.* Her. Liyah.

Treacherously, she felt her defences weaken.

Up close, he still towered over her, even in heels.

His jaw was dark with stubble. He was so broad that he blocked everything else out.

And then he said, 'You really wouldn't mind?'

Liyah couldn't think straight. 'Wouldn't mind what?'

'If I slept with another woman?'

A raging hungry beast reared up inside her, and his scent and proximity made her defences crumble to dust. She had an image of him at the oasis, watching her emerge from the water, holding his hand out to her. Something very elemental moved through her.

This man was hers.

And right then she couldn't remember why it was so important to fight that.

'I would mind.'

Had she growled as she'd said that? She couldn't be sure, but she didn't care, because Sharif had his hands on her waist again and was tugging her towards him. It was only when their bodies touched that she realised she was shaking from the need overflowing inside her.

He went still. 'This doesn't change anything, Liyah. We're just letting our mutual chemistry burn out or else it'll drive us crazy. But that's all it is. It doesn't change what this marriage is.'

Not a marriage. A business arrangement.

'I know,' Liyah said, hoping she didn't sound too desperate. 'That's fine with me.'

She didn't want anything more either. She wanted her freedom. Independence. She certainly didn't want to risk her heart after a lifetime of learning that those who were meant to love you most either left you or rejected you. Or asked you to sacrifice your freedom for theirs.

This had nothing to do with emotions. It was desire. Physical. She could handle that.

To make sure he understood, she said, 'I want you, Sharif.'

As if a switch had been flicked, he muttered something guttural and dug his hands into her hair, clasping her head, tipping her face up to his. Liyah gripped his arms and his muscles bunched under her palms. Her legs nearly gave way and she had to lock them to stay standing.

When his mouth covered hers electricity shot into her veins and straight to every erogenous point. She was suddenly ravenous, reaching up and straining to get closer. There were too many clothes in the way. She scrabbled for Sharif's waistcoat, pushing it off, dislodging his hands. Then his bow-tie and shirt.

When his chest was bare she pulled back and put her hands on him. He was warm and vital. The hair tickled her palms. His heart was thudding heavily. She felt drunk. Even though she'd barely touched her champagne earlier.

'You… I want to see you, Liyah.'

She turned around and pulled her hair over her shoulder, presenting him with her back. He pulled down her zip, his fingers stopping just above her buttocks. The dress loosened around her chest. Sharif came close behind her. She shivered when his bare chest met her back and his arms went around her, his hands cupping and measuring the weight of her breasts. She moaned with need, her head falling back against his shoulder.

He caught her jaw, tipped her face up so that his mouth could meet hers as he found and caught a nipple between his fingers, lightly pinching and rolling it until Liyah couldn't breathe with her need. She twisted in his arms, facing him again, her hands scrabbling for his belt, undoing it, opening a button, pushing his trousers and briefs down over his hips.

They were still standing in the foyer of the apartment. They'd barely moved two feet. But she didn't even notice. She took his rigid flesh in her hand, feeling the size and weight of him, hearing his sharp sucked-in breath, revelling in a momentary feeling of power.

He took her hand away. She looked up and quivered inwardly at the expression on his face.

'No time to play. I need you now.'

He backed her up until her shoulders hit the door with a soft thud. The wood was cool against her heated flesh. He crowded her and she revelled in it, wrapping her arms around his neck, rubbing her breasts against his chest.

She felt curiously emotional in the midst of this onslaught of sensation. She'd thought she'd never see him again after that night at the oasis. And then there'd been the shock of discovering he was her husband, and the belief that he didn't want her again.

But that was all incinerated to dust now, under his mouth. She squeezed her eyes shut to avoid him seeing anything of her feelings.

After a deep, drugging kiss, he broke away to press his mouth against her skin, her shoulder, her neck, and then down. He lifted her breast and cupped it so that he could zero in on her throbbing nipple, sucking and pulling the taut peak into his mouth, nipping with his teeth until Liyah was squirming, her every nerve-ending on fire.

Suddenly Sharif reared back and said throatily, 'Put your legs around me.'

Liyah kicked off her shoes, and when he lifted her up she locked her legs around his hips. The centre of her body came into contact with his, the flimsy lace of her underwear no barrier. She bit her lip, fighting not to beg because she knew that he was going to ease the burning ache in her core right here, right now.

He reached between them and she heard a faint rip. Her underwear. She didn't care. He guided the head of his erection to her centre, to where she was weeping with need. He looked at her as he teased her, lubricating his own body with the slick evidence of her desire.

And then, just when she thought she could take no more, he thrust deep, stealing her breath and her sanity. She was so primed that it took only a few deep, hard strokes to push her over the edge, and then her body clamped around Sharif's as he found his own release, his hips jerking in the aftermath of a storm so fast and intense they couldn't move for long moments.

Slowly Liyah began to put the shattered pieces of herself back together. She became aware of Sharif's arm around her waist. His other hand was by her head, against the door. His face was buried in her neck, his breath uneven. Warm. Their hearts were pounding. Skin slick with perspiration.

Sharif lifted his head slowly. Liyah couldn't look away. She was aware that she'd never been more exposed, but she couldn't seem to care.

To her surprise, Sharif caught a piece of wayward hair and tucked it behind her ear. He said, 'Okay?'

She felt emotional again. She nodded quickly in a bid to distract him. To distract herself. 'Fine.'

When Sharif put her down gently, Liyah winced at the loss of connection. Her dress was ruched up to her waist and the top had fallen down, baring her breasts. Her underwear was strewn on the ground, as were her bag, Sharif's jacket and shirt and tie. Her shoes...

She pulled her dress up and bent to pick up her underwear. When she reached for the shoes Sharif took her hand and pulled her up.

'Leave them.'

He'd pulled his trousers up, but the button was still open. He looked thoroughly disreputable and dangerous, and Liyah's over-stimulated body pulsed back into life.

He tugged her behind him. She followed on legs like jelly, holding her dress up. 'Where are we going?'

He looked back at her and smiled wickedly. 'To continue discussing this renegotiation.'

Sharif stood looking down at the sleeping form of his wife for a long moment. She was sprawled on her front, one arm raised. He could see the plump flesh of one breast. Her lush bottom. Those long legs that had wrapped around him like a vice, holding him, pulling him so deep inside her that he'd seen stars.

His blood ran thickly in his veins in an overload of pleasure. He'd never experienced this after sex.

Liar.

He made a face to acknowledge the fact that he had. Once before. With the same woman.

The confirmation that her effect on him was still as

potent was disturbing. Sex for him was usually a momentary thing, a passing release of energy. This was
something else. Something he didn't want to investigate.

Because surely it would burn out.

It was nothing more than extraordinary chemistry.

He assured himself that he was merely taking advantage of an unprecedented situation—the fact that
he wanted his convenient wife. If anything, not having
to feign intimacy would help his cause. And, more importantly, it would defuse her ability to distract him.

But then Sharif became aware that he was still standing there, captivated by his sleeping wife. So much for
not being distracted. He'd been due at a meeting half
an hour ago.

With a scowl marring his features, and his body resisting leaving her behind, Sharif left the bedroom.

When Liyah woke she felt as if she was floating in a
soft silken ocean. Every limb was heavy and utterly
relaxed. There was a hum in her blood. A hum of satisfaction. But also of…hunger.

Her eyes snapped open as a rush of X-rated memories assailed her from last night. Sharif bringing her to
his room, stripping her bare before stripping off his re-
maining clothes. Laying her on the bed and spreading
her legs so that he could put his mouth to her…

Liyah put a hand over her face and groaned softly.
She'd been so wanton. Begging for more. He'd made
love to her over and over again. Until they'd been limp
with exhaustion and pink trails had coloured the Paris
sky outside.

She opened her eyes again. And now it was bright

daylight. She felt disorientated. She was not used to sleeping in.

Not used to being ravished.

She lifted her head and looked around. The room was empty. She spread out an arm. The bed beside her was cold. Sharif had probably left hours ago. She felt at a disadvantage. Her skin prickled and she pulled the cover over her naked body, suddenly feeling a little exposed—as if instinctively aware that he'd observed her while she slept.

Now she was being silly. Sharif Marchetti was not a man who lingered over his lovers. His absence was proof of that.

Hating feeling at such a disadvantage, and feeling like a sloth, Liyah got up and grabbed a robe from the back of Sharif's bathroom door. It dwarfed her and it smelled of him. She resisted the urge to hold it up to her face and breathe deep, and gathered up her dress and shoes before creeping back to her own room as if she'd been engaged in some illicit activity.

Sharif watched Liyah from the other side of the room. They were in one of Paris's famous atelier salons, where painstakingly intricate work went into creating the most stunning dresses in the world, primarily for haute couture. Clothes that could literally only be afforded by the very few and very privileged. Clothes that were often likened to pieces of art rather than fashion.

He'd found himself quite unintenionally calling Liyah to see if she wanted to come here with him.

She was wearing a long rust-coloured corduroy dress, with buttons down the front and a brown leather belt. Leather high-heeled boots. Her hair was tied back, showing off that amazing bone structure.

She looked the part of wife of the CEO of the Marchetti Group. Casual, but elegant and stylish. And she was listening intently to an older French woman—one of the typically expert seamstresses who worked behind the scenes to create the astonishing confections that would be worn down a runway at some point in the future.

Growing bored of the conversation he was meant to be listening to, about stats and figures and projections—this kind of very specialised work was at constant risk of being eroded by newer inventions and ways of creating clothes—Sharif gravitated towards Liyah, telling himself that it had nothing to do with the pull he still felt in his blood, that hadn't cooled since last night.

He couldn't remember a night of such unbridled passion. He had been insensible to everything but the woman under him. One orgasm had led to another until he'd been too exhausted to move.

Their night at the oasis had been a mere prelude to the most amazing chemistry he'd ever experienced. And the fact that it was happening with a woman who was his wife…was mind-blowing.

Liyah was wearing special gloves to handle a dress, and speaking to the woman in French, exclaiming over the work. The woman was obviously pleased with Liyah's praise, her cheeks pink with pride.

'C'est vraiment incroyable...'

Liyah looked up at Sharif as he came to stand beside her. An electric frisson sizzled up his spine. Her eyes widened as if she felt it too. The buttons at the front of her dress were fastened just low enough for him to see the curve of her breasts, the V in her cleavage.

It was an effort to drag his gaze up and see that Liyah was speaking.

'Martine was telling me that it's taken six months to make this dress.'

Sharif tore his gaze off Liyah and smiled at the woman. 'Your work, as always, is sublime, Martine.'

The woman went even pinker now.

He took Liyah's hand and the hungry beast inside him seemed to calm somewhat. A niggling observation he chose not to investigate.

Just as he was bringing her back to where he'd been talking with the design team at the house, the head designer appeared in their path.

He exclaimed dramatically, 'Who is this creature?' while looking at Liyah.

Sharif felt his hackles rise—which seemed to happen a lot lately, whenever someone looked at Liyah. 'This is my wife, Liyah.'

'You are exquisite.'

The man walked around her, looking her up and down. She looked slightly bemused. Then he introduced himself to Liyah and took her hand, pressing a kiss to the back of it and bowing theatrically.

Liyah smiled at the dramatics.

Sharif's hackles went even higher.

The designer looked at Sharif. 'I have been looking for the right person to try on one of my newest designs and now I've met her. Please can I borrow your wife for ten minutes?'

Sharif wanted to growl at the man. *No.* But he knew

he was being totally irrational. The designer was paying Liyah a huge compliment, and he would look petty if he refused.

'Of course.' He turned to Liyah. 'If you don't mind?'

She looked a little uncertain, but she shrugged. 'Not at all—if it'll fit?'

The designer looked excited as he grabbed Liyah's hand and pulled her away from Sharif. He said, 'Oh, it'll fit—I know it will. And you will look fabulous. Then all we have to do is convince your husband to let you wear it in public.'

The first thing that erupted into Sharif's head when Liyah emerged from behind a curtain some twenty minutes or so later was that there was no way in hell she would ever appear in public wearing the most provocative outfit he'd ever seen.

It was moulded to every dip, hollow and curve of her body. Being round-necked and long-sleeved didn't make it any more demure.

The designer stood beside him and said in an awed voice, 'Have you ever seen anything more perfect?'

Sharif got out a strangled, 'What is it?'

'A sequinned zebra print catsuit.'

Liyah looked like a feline goddess. Even the fact that she didn't have the confidence of a model couldn't detract from the overall look.

Sharif's phone rang at that moment and he picked it out of his pocket, actually relieved that he had a moment's distraction from the vision in front of him. It was his chief strategic advisor, reminding him of an invitation to go to the opening of a new nightclub in Paris that evening.

Sharif had dismissed the invitation originally, because he loathed nightclubs. But his advisor was saying now, 'I know you don't usually go to events like this, but the club is owned by Felipe Sanchez—who we both know is worth keeping an eye on because he's starting to encroach on our territory…buying up designer labels and luxury brands that are outside our sphere of interest. But, as we know well, today's undesirable brand could become tomorrow's behemoth. We need to keep an eye on him. If you went to the opening, perhaps your presence…and your wife's…would eclipse some of Felipe's bid to grab publicity. I don't think I need to tell you that Princess Aaliyah is attracting a lot of press attention. They want more of her…'

As much as Sharif hated the notion of doing anything in response to someone else's provocation, he knew his advisor was right. The last thing he needed was a rival upsetting his plans before he was ready to unveil them to the world. And, as much as he didn't want anyone else to see Liyah as she was right now, he knew that if she appeared in public in this outfit, on his arm, an eclipse would be guaranteed.

If not a nucelar meltdown…

That evening, central Paris

Liyah was naked in public. Well, not literally naked. But she felt naked—because she was so far out of her comfort zone that it was both terrifying and exhilarating at the same time.

She was wearing the catsuit she'd tried on earlier in the atelier and the material was gossamer-light, heightening her feeling of being exposed. She and Sharif had just stepped out of his car. Before them lay a red carpet, populated by well-known faces from the music world, actors and actresses… And at the other end of the carpet were the glittering lights of the newly opened nightclub. The pounding drum and bass of the music could be felt even from here.

Up till now, attending an event with Sharif had been a sophisticated and elegant affair. Tonight was something very different. Edgier, younger. Sharif wore a plain black suit and a black shirt, unbuttoned. Liyah saw a girl walk past wearing what looked like two slivers of silver lamé held together by pins.

Suddenly she didn't feel so naked, and when Sharif took her hand and said, 'Okay?' she looked at him and nodded, aware that for the first time she wanted to please him.

When he'd asked if she'd mind wearing this outfit to an event this evening, her first instinct had been to say *No way*. It was the kind of thing she would never wear in a million years. It had been one thing to try it on for the designer—but another entirely to wear it publicly, as if this was the kind of outfit, or event she took in her stride. When underneath it all, in spite of her metamorphosis over the last few whirlwind weeks, she was still just a nerdy academic who loved the outdoors and travelling and learning about the world.

But that wasn't entirely true. Because with Sharif she was discovering that she had a whole other side to her that she'd never explored before. A side that had been shut down after the experience with her first lover in

England. A side that revelled in wearing something so provocative even as it terrified her.

Because she knew it had an incendiary effect on Sharif …

After their visit to the atelier he'd accompanied her back to the apartment, and the evidence of just how provocative he'd found the catsuit had had him growling instructions into his phone to clear his schedule before taking Liyah to his room and making love to her with a hunger that had inflamed her. The after-effects lingered in her blood even now.

But now the world exploded in their faces as the wall of paparazzi caught sight of them and en masse trained their lenses on Liyah, in the glittering sequinned catsuit.

A couple of hours later, Liyah was sleepily curled into Sharif's side in the back of the car. to her surprise Sharif had deigned to stay for longer than a nanosecond at the club. He'd even—shock, horror—gone onto the dance floor with her. She smiled to herself at the memory.

Her ears were still ringing slightly after the loud music, so she was only half aware that Sharif was talking to someone on the phone. But then her ears pricked up.

'It worked very well,' he was saying. 'Felipe's reaction alone made it worthwhile attending.' And then, 'There are? Already? Send them to me.'

Sharif terminated the conversation.

Liyah sat up. He was looking at his phone and she saw an image of herself. She looked closer, not feeling sleepy any more. 'Is that me? From tonight?'

Sharif angled the phone towards her. There were a

few images of them on the red carpet. And also some grainy ones from inside the club. A rush of hot exposure came back to her as she saw herself straining closer to Sharif on the dance floor, her arms twined around his neck, every point of their bodies touching. She was looking up at him and she looked utterly besotted.

'The pictures from tonight are already going viral. I think it's safe to say that the news of the opening of Felipe Sanchez's new club will fade into insignificance next to the pictures of you in that catsuit.'

'Who is Felipe Sanchez?'

'Someone who needs to be monitored. He's not a threat now, but if unchecked he could become one.'

Liyah felt sick as the evening took on another connotation. 'So he's a rival?'

Sharif said, 'You could describe him as that.'

'And this evening was about deflecting attention from him,' Liyah surmised flatly.

She handed back Sharif's phone and moved away, towards the car door. The rush of betrayal was all too familiar. Along with the sense of exposure. And self-recrimination for having thought for a second that tonight had been some kind of date.

She said, 'I'm under no illusions that this is a real relationship, but I would appreciate it if you would inform me the next time you're intending to use me as a pawn in your quest for world domination.'

Sharif felt the bite of his conscience. He heard the hurt in Liyah's voice. Impossible not to. And the fact that he was so attuned to another human being, probably for the first time since his mother had died, was an uncomfortable sensation.

She said accusingly, 'That's *my* image that's going to be plastered all over the internet tomorrow.'

'Your image has already caused quite a stir on the internet,' Sharif pointed out.

'Yes, but not while wearing a sequinned zebra print catsuit.'

Sharif felt the distance between them like a physical thing. He didn't like it. He wanted to reach for her, but knew not to.

'You look amazing. That's why you're currently breaking the internet.'

'Maybe I don't want to break the internet.'

Sharif shook his head. 'You have no idea how stunning you are, do you? Who taught you that you weren't beautiful?'

He could see Liyah flinch minutely, and he wanted to curl his hand into a fist and punch someone.

'Tell me again about that guy you were with.'

'He wasn't anyone important.'

'He made you feel insignificant?'

He saw her swallow. When she spoke her voice was husky.

'He was just a guy at my university. As you can imagine, coming from Taraq, I was less…worldly than most other girls my age. He singled me out—made me feel special. I thought he was attractive, but now I can see that I was confused by the attention he was showing me. I was used to standing out because of my height and my colouring. But he seemed to see beyond that.'

'What happened?' Sharif had to curb the violent urge he felt at the thought of such a man uncovering her sensual beauty and not appreciating it.

Liyah shrugged, looked down at her lap. 'He had a bet with his friends that he could get me into bed after one date. I… I was eager to live a modern life. I wanted to lose my virginity, to feel mature, independent…' She looked up. 'He won the bet.'

Sharif emitted a crude Italian swear word in response. He reached for Liyah, unable to resist any longer. She was tense, but she moved closer. She was sinuous under the delicate fabric and he had to curb the urge to rip it from her body there and then. He'd already given in to the storm of lust this bodysuit had unleashed earlier.

'He was an idiot. And he didn't deserve the gift you gave him.'

Liyah's heart hitched. She didn't doubt Sharif's sincerity.

She couldn't believe she'd told him of her humiliation, but the hurt she'd been feeling upon discovering how he'd manipulated and orchestrated this evening was fading into insignificance next to the way he was looking at her right now.

His hands found where her hair was slicked back into the bun and he undid it, letting it unravel down her back and over her shoulders. He cupped her face in his hands.

'Never let anyone make you feel small, Liyah,' he said. 'You are stunning, and you have a power that I don't think you even recognise fully yet. You're formidable.'

Liyah's heart did more than hitch this time. She quickly tried to negate it. Remind herself who she was with—a man who undoubtedly was a master at complimenting needy lovers. The thought of *lovers* made her want to hiss and spit…

'You don't have to say that.'

'I know,' he said simply. 'But it's true. And if the thought of those pictures really upsets you then I'll have my team take care of removing them.'

Liyah blinked. 'You would do that?'

He nodded. 'I could certainly limit them.'

Liyah asked, 'Will they be good for your business?'

Sharif hesitated for a moment, and then he said, 'In a word? Yes. More than you know.'

'Then it's okay—leave them out there.'

'Are you sure? We have a window to limit this right now, but if we wait till morning it'll be gone.'

Liyah shook her head. She put her hands on Sharif's chest. 'No, it's okay. I know you're not used to answering to anyone. But next time… Just let me know. Okay?'

Sharif's mouth tipped up on one side. 'Deal. Now, will you let me make it up to you?'

'How?'

'Like this…'

He pressed the button to make the privacy screen go up between them and the driver, and then he reached for the zip at the back of the suit, pulling it down so that he could peel the suit over her shoulders, down her arms and away from her chest, exposing her breasts to his hungry gaze.

'Sharif…' Liyah said weakly as he bent forward and cupped one breast.

He looked at her and arched a brow. 'Yes?'

'We shouldn't…not here.'

He blew on her nipple, before flicking out his tongue

to taste the hard tip. It hardened even more. Liyah bit her lip.

'Do you want me to stop?'

Never. Liyah was on fire.

She moved back, drawing Sharif with her so he loomed over her supine body. 'No. Don't stop.'

He smiled and it was wicked. 'Your wish, Mrs Marchetti, is my command.'

And even in the midst of Sharif's lovemaking Liyah knew that something had happened here in the back of the car. Something that she didn't want to look at too closely. Because she sensed that, far from renegotiating this marriage as a purely physical thing, they'd moved way beyond that now.

Or, fatally, *she* had.

CHAPTER NINE

Two days later, London

LIYAH LOOKED OUT at a spectacular bird's eye view of London—naturally. Sharif's apartment was the penthouse of one of London's most exclusive hotels. On one side was the Presidential Suite and on the other Sharif's apartment.

Liyah could see the iconic Tower Bridge nearby, and all the way up the Thames to the London Eye.

As per Sharif's schedule, which was emailed to her now, they were here for the engagement party of Sasha and her fiancé. Sasha was Maks's younger sister, but no relation to Sharif or Nikos as she'd had a different father.

Liyah was curious to meet Maks and his wife—and Sasha. And to glean more nuggets of information about Sharif.

She still felt a little tender after Paris. Tender from the revelation that she could no longer ignore.

She'd fallen in love with Sharif. And it had happened in spite of everything she'd experienced that had made her want to protect herself from such vulnerability. She knew how those who were meant to love you most either left you or just…didn't love you.

It had happened with the speed and impact of an unstoppable train. And she knew why. Because, contrary to that first time, when Liyah had felt 'seen' by her lover, she now knew she had not been. That had been wishful thinking on her part—a need to justify allowing someone the ultimate intimacy. But with Sharif… she really did feel seen.

Literally, in her first interaction with him, she'd been naked.

But it was more than that. She felt an affinity with him that she'd never felt with anyone else. Not even her sister. She saw a kindred spirit in his self-isolation. His lone wolfness. It resonated in her because she'd always been alone too.

Now, for the first time in her life she didn't feel alone.

And it was so dangerous—because for Sharif this was still very much physical. And she sensed that, while her own defences had ultimately been too weak to withstand him, his defences were far stronger.

His life was built around avenging his mother's betrayal and death. He hadn't spelt it out like that, but she'd guessed it. He had a singular ambition and Liyah was a momentary diversion, helping him to that end.

But what of that end? What would happen if and when he did avenge his mother? Would he have peace then? Or move on to the next challenge?

'Ready?'

Liyah turned around, startled out of her reverie. Sharif stood in the doorway to the palatial lounge in a black tuxedo. She sucked in a breath, still not used to the punch to her gut every time she saw him.

'Yes, I'm ready.'

This evening she was wearing a black silk dress. It had a high neck and long sleeves, and fell just below her knee. A gold belt cinched in her waist and the flowing fabric. It was paired with black high heels. She felt covered up and relatively demure, which was welcome after the other night in Paris and the catsuit.

The morning after that night at the club she'd woken to find it torn and in tatters. Much to her mortification. It hadn't survived intact after Sharif's lovemaking in the car, and then when they'd arrived back at the apartment, the zip had got stuck and Sharif had ripped the fabric asunder. Not that Liyah had objected at the time.

But, considering how viral those pictures of her in the suit had gone after that night, Liyah figured the designer had got his value from it. She just prayed he wouldn't ask for its return.

'You've left your hair down,' Sharif commented.

Liyah walked over to him, growing warm from the heated look in his gaze. 'Did you want me to put it up?'

He shook his head and curved a hand around the back of her neck, tugging her towards him. He pressed a swift kiss to her mouth, and even that had Liyah moaning softly. Since the other night, it was as if any restraint was a thing of the past.

They'd even made love on the plane on the way from Paris to London. A flight that had taken less than two hours.

When he touched her like this, or made love to her,

it was easy to pretend to herself that it was just physical, but she knew it wasn't. For her.

The engagement party was being held in one of London's most iconic hotels near Hyde Park. When they arrived in the main lobby, Sharif was approached by a man Liyah had never seen before. He introduced the man to her as the Marchetti Group's head of European PR. Liyah smiled, but lost interest as the two men engaged in a conversation about strategy.

She saw an eye-catching modern painting on the wall nearby and wandered over to take a closer look. When she felt a presence close by she looked up with a smile on her face, expecting to see Sharif, but it wasn't Sharif, and it took her a second to place who it was.

The man put out his hand. 'We met in New York, shortly after your wedding. I believe it was your first public event with your husband?'

Liyah instinctively recoiled, remembering the reporter who had confronted Sharif at that first event at the Metropolitan Museum. 'Mr Callaghan, isn't it?'

He smiled unctuously and she recoiled even further.

'Well remembered, Mrs Marchetti.' He took a card out of his pocket and held it towards her. 'I just wanted to give you my contact details, in case you ever feel you want to share what life is like on the inside of the world's most successful—'

The card was plucked out of Callaghan's hand before Liyah could touch it. She breathed a sigh of relief as Sharif pulled her close. His voice was icy.

'Aren't you a little far from home, Callaghan? And this is a private family event.'

The man stepped back and held his hands up in a

mock show of humility. 'What can I say? I just happened to be in London at the same time.'

Sharif made a rude sound. 'Clear off, Callaghan.
You're not welcome.'

Sharif led Liyah away, and threw the card into a bin
as they passed through the lobby. She felt a prickling
at the back of her neck, as if the man was still staring
after them, but when she looked around he was gone.

In the elevator, Sharif said tightly, 'What did he
want?'

'He wanted to give me his contact details. He seems
to be looking for a story.'

She looked up at Sharif. His jaw was tight.

'There is no story.'

The elevator doors were opening now, and in a bid to
try and move on from that unsettling encounter Liyah
asked, 'What does Sasha's fiancé do?'

'His name is Dante Danieli. He's an award-winning
photographer and film-maker.'

They stepped into a luxuriously decorated function
room at the top of the hotel. Staff came and took their
overcoats. Sharif took her hand and led her into the
room, which oozed elegant sophistication, dressed in
a theme of silver and grey and pink, with huge exotic
blooms as centrepieces on the tables.

A waiter approached with a tray of champagne.
Sharif took two glasses and handed her one.

Almost immediately Liyah recognised Maggie and
Nikos, who had spotted them and were coming over.
She was surprised at how pleased she was to see them
again, greeting them warrmly.

Maggie said, 'I saw those pictures of you in that one-

piece suit and I'm so jealous.' She pointed to her growing belly. 'I don't think I'll ever fit into anything like
that ever again. Not that I would even be able to pull it
off! You looked amazing.'

Liyah blushed. She felt Sharif's arm come around
her waist.

'Didn't she?'

The warm feeling grew as they chatted companion-
ably with Nikos and Maggie, and Liyah noticed that
Sharif seemed less tense than he had before.

And then another tall man approached, with a petite
woman by his side. He had dark blond colouring. Short
hair. Gorgeous. Maks Marchetti.

'Sharif. I see that you're finally having some fun.' He
looked at Liyah, smiling, 'And this must be the reason
why you've taken that stick out of your—'

'Maks!' his wife exclaimed. She put a hand out to
Liyah. 'Hi, I'm Zoe. It's so nice to meet you.'

Liyah shook her hand and Maks winked at her.
'Don't mind me. I just like to wind Sharif up at every
opportunity, and it's nice to see him discover he's mor-
tal too.'

Sharif made a rude sound beside her. Liyah shook
Maks's hand, momentarily mesmerised by his grey
eyes. Very different from Nikos and Sharif. She sneaked
a glance between the men as they chatted. Each one
as tall and imposing as the other. They packed quite
a punch.

Liyah was drawn into a conversation with Maggie
and Zoe. It felt quite natural, and she was unable to stay
shy for long. They were both so down to earth. Zoe was
pregnant too—almost out of her first trimester. She was

very attractive, with honey-blonde shoulder-length hair. She had scars on her face that intrigued Liyah, but they didn't detract from her prettiness.

It was more than a little overwhelming to feel as if she was part of this group of people. And then she felt an acute pang as she acknowledged the fact that she wouldn't be part of it for long. She and Sharif would divorce and she wouldn't see them again.

Maks and Zoe excused themselves to go and check on Sasha, who Liyah guessed was the tall woman near the dais. She looked like Maks—a feminine version. Tall. Blonde hair. She was stunning. Wearing a blush-coloured strapless dress. Diamonds sparkled at her throat and wrists, and even from here Liyah could see the huge diamond on her finger.

A man joined Sasha. He was in a tuxedo. Tall and broad. Messy dark hair. He was very masculine, and savagely handsome. He pulled her to his side and whispered something in her ear that made her giggle and blush. She looked happy. Another couple truly in love…?

A dart of envy pierced Liyah before she could stop it. And, suddenly feeling a little too vulnerable to be around Sharif, in case he spotted it, Liyah made her excuses and walked over to where some French doors were partially open. She went outside to the terrace. It was cold, but the first hints of spring on the way could be felt. New life…

London sparkled under the moon. Vibrant and glamorous. It had always been her favourite city. But the desert… That was where her heart lay.

She was so wrapped up in her thoughts she didn't

hear Sharif join her, but she felt him when her pulse inexplicably picked up.

'Penny for them?'

She looked at him, so tall and vital and handsome in his tuxedo. She shrugged and looked back out over the view. 'I was just thinking of cities…and the desert. I miss it. I think it's where I feel most at home, even though it can be such an inhospitable place.'

Sharif placed his hands on the terrace wall. 'You miss your horse and your bird?'

She nodded. 'I feel free in the desert. Totally at peace.'

He turned and leant against the terrace wall, facing her. 'When my father sent those mercenaries to kidnap me I blamed the desert for a long time. As if it had somehow betrayed me by not protecting me.' He grimaced. 'Obviously I know better, but that's how the desert is for me—like a living organism.' His mouth quirked. 'I've since forgiven it.'

Liyah said, 'It's so vibrant and full of life, but it can turn on you in an instant. I got caught in a sandstorm once—scariest experience of my life.'

They stood in silence for a moment.

Then Liyah said, 'I know you said you took on your father's business because it was your due, and your brothers', and because you wanted to make something of it, but I can't imagine it was easy to take over from a man you hated so much.'

'It wasn't,' Sharif admitted. 'I despised it at first. Because I despised him and anything he touched. I thought his business was a vacuous world, full of vain people. I thought it had no value. Until I had access to the accounts and saw the spreadsheets. At first it was very much a means to an end for me—rebuilding it. But over time, as I got to know more, I came to appreciate the industry. I think there's a place for enduring brands in the world. And for fashion and art. We provide something aspirational. Inspirational. And I think we can do a lot of good in changing things for the better. In terms of the environment. Inclusivity. Diversity. Art and design and creativity is what civilises us. If that disappears, or becomes eroded, we lose something very valuable.'

Liyah stayed silent, willing Sharif to continue.

'We had an intern in one of our offices from South Africa. He grew up in poverty in the townships. His mother cleaned in the big rich houses and she used to bring home copies of *Vogue*. For a young gay boy, who literally had nothing else, those magazines were a portal to another world, where he could fantasise about being someone else.'

Sharif looked at Liyah, and pride was visible on his face.

'He won Men's Designer of the Year at the fashion awards a few months ago.'

Liyah smiled. 'I love that story.'

People started clapping and cheering inside.

'We're missing the announcement,' she said. 'We should go back in.'

But Sharif caught her hand and stopped her, pulling her towards him until they were touching. 'I prefer it out here.'

'Do you, now?'

'Yes… I do.

He took off his jacket and placed it over her shoulders, before tugging on it so that she came even closer. Surrounded by his smell and his body heat, Liyah cast aside all her concerns and gave herself up to the moment.

Because she knew that when the time came all she would have to remember would be moments like this.

Later that night—much later—when they returned to the apartment, to Sharif's bedroom, Liyah wasn't prepared for the urgency that gripped her as soon as Sharif put his hands on her face and tipped it up so he could kiss her.

She realised she'd been waiting for this moment all evening.

She was ravenous.

She scrabbled to undo his clothes as his hands moved over her body, undoing her dress, taking it off her. His kisses stole her sanity. She pulled back, dizzy, to see Sharif shed his clothes. A button popped. Liyah felt like giggling, but it was drowned out by the rush of blood to her head when she saw Sharif's magnificent body bared.

He was like a warrior. And she wanted to honour him.

She dropped to her knees in front of him and heard his surprised huff of air. 'Liyah, what are you—?'

But she couldn't resist that straining column of flesh. She wanted to taste him. The very essence of him. She wrapped her hand around him and heard him suck in a breath, whistling through his teeth.

He put his hands on her head, his fingers clamping tight as she inexpertly explored the thick, rigid flesh, running her tongue around the head before putting her mouth around him fully.

* * *

Sharif's legs were shaking…his hands trembling. He didn't recognise himself right now, having gone from civilised to carnal beast in about zero to ten seconds. It had taken all his restraint not to leave the party early, drag Liyah back to the apartment like some hormonal schoolboy.

He'd actually fantasised about her doing this, and now he was straining with the effort it took to keep his hips still.

Eventually it became too much. As much as he wanted to find oblivion in Liyah's far too tempting mouth, he wanted to be buried deep inside her more. And that was a revelation he refused to look at now—usually this form of release suited him just fine, feeling like a lesser form of intimacy.

He pulled back and Liyah looked up at him, her eyes unfocused. Her hair was wild and tumbling over her shoulders, almost obscuring her breasts.

Sharif couldn't even speak. He just pulled her up and lifted her, carrying her over to the bed before laying her down. He felt off-centre and, despite the clawing need to plunge deep and find satisfaction right now, he forced himself to go slow, to prove that he hadn't lost it completely.

Liyah was still dizzy from the headiness of what she'd just done, from how it had felt and tasted to have him in her mouth. At her mercy. She'd felt the tension in his hips, the way his hands had trembled in her hair. But now he seemed intent on proving that any notion she might have that she had the upper hand was sadly misplaced.

He came between her legs and pushed them apart, moving his big hands up to her thighs, spreading them even wider as he bent down, pressing kisses along the tender inner skin, his breath feathering closer and closer to the centre of her body, where her flesh pulsed.

And then he put his mouth on her flesh. She arched her back and grabbed the sheet with both hands, straining to contain the pleasure building at her core. But it was impossible. One flick of his wicked tongue and she was tumbling over the edge, and her body was still contracting when he reared over her and plunged deep, sending her into another spiral of ecstasy, showing her all too comprehensively who was the expert.

Liyah lay there for a long moment afterwards, her skin cooling and her breathing returning to normal. She was shell-shocked all over again at how this was between them. But surely it would begin to fade? This intense need and desire?

She heard Sharif's breathing return to normal beside her. She wondered if he was thinking the same thing.

And then he surprised her by saying abruptly, 'Actually, Callaghan isn't entirely wrong. I do have plans for the Marchetti Group. My plan is to destroy it.'

Callaghan. The reporter who had followed them to London. Liyah turned on her side to face him, shocked. 'What?'

Sharif didn't look at her. 'I'm going to reduce the Marchetti Group to nothing. That's what I've been working towards. Building it up until it's powerful beyond anything my father could ever have imagined and then selling it off, piece by piece, until his legacy no longer exists. All the success he garnered off the backs of the women he seduced and stole from will be forgotten.'

Liyah went very still. 'But…but all that stuff you told me earlier about appreciating the industry…'

'This won't affect the industry at large. It'll cause a few waves, yes, but the brands will continue to exist. Just not under the Marchetti name.'

'But what if they don't survive without your support?' Liyah thought of the women who worked in the atelier in Paris.

'That's part of my reasoning in making sure we're in a strong position. All the brands and labels will be desirable lucrative concerns.'

Liyah came up on one elbow. 'What about your brothers? They don't know about your plans, do they?'

Sharif threw back the covers and got up from the bed in a fluid movement. He walked over to a set of drawers and pulled out a pair of sweat pants, put them on. They hung low on his hips as he walked over to the window, arms folded.

Liyah sat up, pulling her knees up to her chest. Feeling cold all of a sudden.

Eventually he said, 'No, they don't know.'

'Because you don't trust them?'

He turned around. 'In a word, no. Even if we do have an accord now, I can't say for certain that they wouldn't go against me—and I can't let that happen. Not when I'm so close. They hated our father as much as I did. Nikos's mother committed suicide because of him. Domenico made Maks's and his sister's life hell when their mother had affairs and ultimately divorced him. I still can't trust that they feel the same way I do, but they won't go without recompense. They'll be billionaires, no matter what.'

'You could talk to them,' Liyah suggested. 'Perhaps not telling them everything but sounding them out? They deserve that, don't they?'

She could see the lines of Sharif's body tense.

'They'd suspect in a second. They're not stupid.'

Liyah pulled up the sheet, feeling exposed. 'I think that you're underestimating them. I think you can trust them. Didn't they come into the group when you suggested it after your father died? They've helped you build it up.'

'They've helped you build it up.'

Sharif was so tightly wound that he felt as if he might crack open. Everything Liyah was saying was hitting him in a place that stung. And he had no idea what had compelled him to tell her any of this. It had started coming out of him before he could stop it.

The truth was that on some level he knew she was right. But he'd been alone for so long, living with his plan to grind his father's name and legacy to dust, that the prospect of it not happening was unconscionable. Too much of a risk.

As if reading his mind, Liyah said softly, 'Would you risk putting a rift between you and your brothers for this?'

'Yes,' he answered, swiftly and emphatically. Except this time it felt hollow.

He'd always figured a rift between him and his brothers would be the unfortunate outcome, but in the past couple of years he and Nikos and Maks had gravitated more and more towards one another. It was easier between them now. He felt…affection.

But he slammed down on all that now. Sentimental nonsense. This whole plan would only succeed with the element of surprise. No one could know.

Liyah got out of the bed, naked. She grabbed Sharif's shirt from where it lay on the floor, slipping into it. It fell to her thighs. Her hair was tousled and she looked thoroughly bedded.

She held the edges of the shirt together. 'I'm going to take a shower and go to bed. Goodnight, Sharif.'

Sharif watched as Liyah left the room, an acrid feeling in his gut. For so long in his life he'd been certain that what he was doing was the right thing. The thing that would finally bring him a sense of vengeance meted out. And then peace.

And yet now all he could see were Liyah's huge eyes, looking at him reproachfully. He could hear her soft voice… *I think you can trust them.*

He turned around to face the window again and cursed. She was making him lose his focus. Damn her. Damn her for not being the wife he'd envisaged—unobtrusive and on the sidelines. Far from that, she was in his bed, under his skin, and every time he looked at her she made his mind go blank with lust.

Damn her for making him want to spill his guts.

And damn her for suddenly making him doubt everything.

Not even a hot shower could warm Liyah up. She wrapped herself in a towelling robe and curled up on the sofa in her bedroom. The extent of Sharif's ambition to avenge his mother and destroy his father even at the risk of alienating his brothers should have shocked her, but it didn't. After all, he'd been prepared to marry a total stranger purely to gain any advantage he could in the run-up to realising his ambition.

She felt cold at the thought of Sharif bearing this heavy, toxic burden for so long. And then she thought if she felt cold, how must *he* feel? He'd been alone for a lot longer than her. Trusting no one.

Obeying an instinct she couldn't ignore, Liyah went back to Sharif's room. He wasn't in bed. And then she heard running water. He was in the shower.

She undid the robe and let it fall to the ground and opened the door. Sharif was standing with his hands on the wall, his head down between his shoulders. There was something so…isolated about his stance that Liyah's heart cracked for him.

She went into the shower and inserted herself between him and the wall. He tensed at first, and those dark eyes with gold around the edges stared at her as if he couldn't believe she was there.

She put her hands on his chest and rose up on her tiptoes, pressing a kiss to his mouth, which was in a hard, flat line. At first he didn't respond. She thought he was going to reject her. But then, as if a dam had burst, Sharif put his arms around her and lifted her up.

She put her legs around him and he leant her back against the wall, running his hand over her breasts, cupping one heavy weight before bending his head to suckle on her eager flesh.

He thrust up into her body, stealing her breath and

her soul. It was slow, deliberate torture, as if he was making her pay for extracting a confession he hadn't wanted to make.

Liyah absorbed it all, and afterwards she wrapped her legs around him even tighter, felt him shudder his release into her body.

Manhattan

Sharif sat in the back of his car and pulled out his mobile phone. He texted Liyah.

I'm on my way home.

Then he stopped, deleted 'home' with a scowl and replaced it.

...to the apartment.

The woman was turning his brain to mush. Since that night in London, almost three weeks ago, they hadn't discussed the subject of his plans again. When Liyah had appeared that night in his shower he'd been consumed with so many tangled emotions that he'd almost told her to leave him alone, but then she'd put her hands on him and he'd lost the will to tell her to go.

It was as if she'd sensed what he needed and taken all of him, absorbing his need to exorcise what was inside him.

The following morning, when he'd woken, he'd felt as close to a sense of peace as he'd ever experienced before in his life.

His phone pinged with a response.

Good for you.

He smiled.

It will be good for me. And for you.

After a couple of seconds:

Promises, promises...

And an eye-roll emoji.

Sharif's blood leapt. He'd make her pay for that. He put his phone away, the smile still on his face.

The past three weeks had been...interesting. He'd had a few events to attend, accompanied by Liyah, and he'd found that as she'd grown more comfortable in his milieu she'd become quite happy to talk to people and not depend on him. If anything, he was the one looking for her now, and he didn't like how used he'd got to having her by his side.

He'd found her in a corner the other evening, talking to a septugenarian professor in Arabic about Taraq.

And one day, at the end of the working day—for normal people—she'd appeared in his office with tickets that she'd bought for a sold-out Broadway show. At first he'd been inclined to refuse, aware that he had enough work to keep him there for hours. But Liyah had looked so crestfallen that he hadn't had the heart to say no.

Sharif couldn't recall the last time he'd gone to a show that hadn't been a premiere, or part of a gala night.

It had been revelatory…how such a regular thing could be so enjoyable. Although in truth he'd got more enjoyment out of watching Liyah enjoy the show. Wearing those glasses that made her look like a sexy academic.

And now he was going home—early, for him—because all day he hadn't been able to get the image of how she'd looked that morning out of his head. Sleepy and sexy. Hair in a wild tangle around her head.

She'd not slept in her own room since they'd returned from London. She shared his room. Which he'd never done with any woman. But he found that he liked seeing her things strewn around the space. Her creams and lotions in the bathroom. Her scent in the air…

He scowled again. He was definitely losing it. The sooner her allure started to fade—as he was sure it would—the better. It was coming closer and closer to the time when he would make the announcement about selling off the Marchetti Group, and he was aware that he was using Liyah as a distraction to avoid thinking about his brothers.

The car pulled up outside the apartment building and Sharif felt his anticipation build as he got nearer to the apartment door. This was also a novelty. Having someone waiting for him. Welcoming him. He'd always been so careful to keep women out of his private space before.

But not Liyah.

As soon as he walked through the door smells assailed him. Smells of Al-Murja. The desert.

He shucked off his jacket and loosened his tie. Explored the apartment, following the smells to the kitchen. He was prepared to see his chef—but it wasn't his chef. It was Liyah. She was wearing jeans and a loose shirt. Bare feet. Hair up in a loose knot.

She was listening to jazz, humming to herself. And the smell of the food made Sharif's mouth water. He smelled spices and lemon. Chicken… Lamb?

He knew he should resist this vision of domesticity. It wasn't what he'd signed up for with this marriage. But it was more seductive than he liked to admit…

Liyah sensed Sharif and whirled around to see him standing in the doorway, leaning against the doorframe. Tie undone, shirt open at the top. Stubbled jaw. Her belly dipped and swooped. Her heart hitched. She felt shy. Which was ridiculous after what they'd done the previous night.

'Hi.'

'You're cooking.'

Liyah smiled. 'I can see why you're CEO—your powers of observation are truly impressive.'

Sharif made a face. He came in, nose twitching. 'What are you cooking?'

'I have a couscous, cherry tomato and herb salad. Lamb and pistachio patties. Harissa chicken. Hummus. Flatbread. Here.'

She handed him some flatbread and hummus. He tasted it.

'That's good. Really good. Where did you learn to cook?'

'I taught myself when I was at university. I felt home-sick for Taraq and I found that cooking meals that reminded me of home helped.'

Sharif said, 'I'll have a quick shower and join you.'

Liyah looked at him. 'You're so sure you're invited?'

Sharif came around the ktichen island and pulled her close, covering her mouth with his. She felt the inevitable spark leap to life between them.

Still there. Not gone yet.

With every kiss now, every night of making love, Liyah was more aware that sooner or later there would come a time when Sharif wouldn't look at her in quite the same way. Wouldn't want her with the same desperation she felt.

He let her go and walked out of the room, leaving Liyah dazed and hungry. And, annoyingly, not for the delicious food she'd made.

Later that evening the movie's credits rolled and Sharif looked down to see Liyah curled up on the couch beside him, snoring softly, glasses askew on her face.

He turned off the TV—another first. Although he had a state-of-the-art media centre installed he rarely, if ever, watched anything except maybe the news.

He felt a sense of something he'd never experienced before, and had to take a few seconds to figure out what it was. *Contentment.* A sense of peace. This whole evening had been…easy. Pleasurable.

Normally, when he didn't have a function to attend, he would spend the evening in his study, with a sense of restlessness buzzing under his skin. A restlessness that was now gone.

He made a face. He was losing it. A little home cooking and his brain was scrambled.

He picked Liyah's glasses off her face and put them to one side. He gathered her into his arms and stood up. She made a sound…her eyes opened. Unfocused. Sleepy. *Sexy.*

She burrowed closer into his chest and Sharif's body reacted to her soft curves. As if he hadn't been in a state of semi-arousal all evening, since he'd returned and found her creating a veritable feast for the taste-buds and senses…

He felt his phone vibrate in his pocket, but by the time he got to the bedroom with Liyah she was awake and wrapping her arms around his neck, pressing open-mouthed kisses to his jaw. He forgot all about checking his phone to see who was looking for him. He had more important things to attend to.

CHAPTER TEN

WHEN LIYAH WOKE UP the following morning she stretched luxuriously, keeping her eyes closed, revelling in the after-effects of Sharif's lovemaking. Blinking blearily, she came up on one elbow and groaned softly when she saw the time on her phone. Nearly midday.

This man had turned her into such a sloth. But it was usually dawn before they were falling asleep, exhausted. Last night had been no different.

A voice from behind her said, 'You're awake.'

Startled, because she'd thought she was alone, Liyah looked over her shoulder to see Sharif at the window. The sun made her squint, but she could see he was fully dressed in a three-piece suit.

She sensed something was wrong and sat up, pulling the sheet to cover her chest, not even sure why she felt instinctively vulnerable all of a sudden.

'Morning… Why aren't you at work?' He was always gone when she woke.

Sharif stepped towards the bed, out of the sunlight. Liyah could see him now and his expression was stony.

'Sharif…what is it?'

He folded his arms. 'Tell me—when do you go into

my study to send your messages to Callaghan? When I've left the apartment? Did seeing him in London give you the idea to go to him with the scoop?'

Liyah wanted to shake her head. Sharif was making no sense.

She sat up properly, clutching the sheet. 'What are you talking about?'

'Come and see for yourself.' He stalked out of the room.

Liyah scrambled to find something to wear, pulling on Sharif's robe, which was hanging on the back of the bathroom door. She didn't even know where he had gone, but she heard the sound of the TV and went into the lounge. Where they had been last night... Until she had fallen asleep and woken in Sharif's arms...

Not now.

The TV was on. A news channel. Sharif stood before it, remote in one hand, his other hand in his pocket. She went and stood beside him. And her innards froze when she realised what she was watching.

As if she couldn't make sense of what the reporter was saying, she read the text that ran at the bottom of the screen.

Sharif Marchetti decides to sell the Marchetti Group... Brothers and fellow board members Nikos and Maks Marchetti...unaware of this development... An emergency meeting of the board is due to take place...

The reporter was talking again. 'Only days ago, Marchetti Group shares were at an all-time high. The company had the Midas touch. It could do no wrong. The question on everyone's lips is why on earth would Sharif Marchetti destroy his own company like this?'

Sharif switched off the TV. He faced Liyah, who was in shock.

'Well?'

She looked at him. She found it hard to speak. To articulate anything. 'How…how did they find out?'

'Really? You're really going to pretend it wasn't you? When Callaghan was the one who got the scoop? You met him—right under my nose in London.'

Liyah's brain felt sluggish as she recalled the man approaching her, trying to give her his card. 'Don't be ridiculous, Sharif. Of course I didn't say anything to him. I didn't even take his card. Why would I say anything?'

'Because you disapprove? Because you feel I'm not being fair to my brothers? Maybe you contacted Nikos and he called Callaghan, hoping to cause a bit of chaos so that I wouldn't go through with it. But I think it was because I gave you privileged information and that was an irresistible currency for you. A way to negotiate the end of our marriage well before time so you could get your precious independence early.'

Liyah's legs felt like jelly. She sat down on the chair behind her. 'That's such a twisted theory… I didn't do this, Sharif. I swear. Whatever I felt about your decision, your motives…that's between you and your brothers.'

'Not any more. It's now between me, my brothers and the entire world. Our stock has plummeted.'

'But…wouldn't this have happened anyway, when you made your announcement?'

'No, it would have been controlled. And I was always

going to tell Nikos and Maks before I did anything. I just wasn't going to involve them until the last moment.' Sharif looked at his watch. 'I have to go. I have to give a press conference this afternoon and then I'm flying to Paris. I don't know when I'll be back.'

He went to walk out of the room and Liyah stood up. Before he disappeared, she said, 'You really believe it was me?'

Sharif stopped. He turned around. 'You're the only one who knew the full extent of my plans. I hadn't even revealed them to my own staff. They were kept in a safe in my office, and the only person who has the code is me.'

Liyah felt sick. Sharif walked out. She stared at the empty space for a long moment. Until she heard Sharif speak with Thomas and then the *ping* of the elevator doors.

He was gone.

Liyah was too numb to process what had just happened. She showered, dressed… Sat on the couch in the lounge and watched Sharif give his press conference a couple of hours later, trying to limit the damage.

Thomas enquired if she wanted to eat, but she had no appetite. At some point she went out and walked the streets for blocks and blocks. Always aware of the security man tailing her. She was almost surprised he was still there…

The speed with which Sharif had turned on her, choosing to believe that she could have possibly— Her stomach roiled.

When she finally returned to the apartment it was

empty. She slept in her own bed for the first time since that first week she'd arrived in Manhattan.

When she woke at dawn she was gritty-eyed. She checked her phone. No calls, no messages.

Days passed in a hazy blur. Liyah saw news reports about how the board of the Marchetti Group were holding crisis meetings. She saw pictures of Nikos and Maks leaving the Paris office, as grim-looking as Sharif, and her heart ached.

They would hate him for not trusting them. The damage would be irreparable.

And then, just like a few months ago, when her sister had called her and begged her for help, Samara needed Liyah again.

And Liyah saw no reason not to go to her—because there was nothing for her here any more.

When Sharif arrived back at his Manhattan apartment all was quiet. He knew Liyah wasn't there. He knew she was in Taraq with her family. Her sister was getting married within the next fortnight, sooner than expected. He'd been invited, but he'd declined.

He shrugged off his jacket and undid his tie. He went straight to his drinks cabinet and poured himself a stiff whisky. Not that whisky had done much to help in the last two weeks since he'd left. But it had blurred the edges and helped him forget the dreams that haunted him most nights. Dreams of *her*. And of treachery.

The liquid burnt its way down his throat. He poured another. The world was in flames around him. Everything he'd worked so hard to achieve was ruined. His fa-

ther was laughing at him from his grave. His mother…
His heart constricted. He'd failed her.

And all because he'd lost his focus. He'd let his brain
migrate to his pants. He'd forgotten a lifetime of lessons
in trusting no one but himself. He'd allowed a siren with
huge green eyes to lull him into a false sense of security. To make a fool out of him.

His phone rang in his pocket and he took it out. Saw
the name. He smiled mirthlessly and restrained himself
from throwing the phone at the window.

He answered it, saying, 'Haven't you done enough
damage, Callaghan? Tell me—did you know that first
night that my wife would betray my trust? Did she come
to you or did you approach her? Actually, I don't even
want to know.'

He emitted an expletive and terminated the call,
throwing the phone down.

It pinged almost immediately, but Sharif ignored it.
He was bone weary.

He walked through his empty apartment, noting that
it was exactly how he remembered, before Liyah had
arrived.

He walked into her room. There was the slightest
hint of her fragrance. But of course—she'd been sharing his room. Because he was the biggest fool on earth.

He went into the dressing room. All the clothes that
he'd purchased for her were hanging up. Shoes lined
up. Jewellery laid out. He was about to leave when he
noticed something and turned back. Her wedding ring.
The second one. It was there. She'd never taken it off
after he'd put it on her finger. But she'd left it behind.

He should be welcoming the sight of it there. Clearly

she'd got the message that the end of this marriage was nigh. But it didn't feel good to see it. He felt as if it was mocking him. For being such a fool.

He turned and walked out, leaving the ring behind.

'You look so beautiful, Sammy—really. Everything will be okay...trust me.'

Liyah's sister was fighting back tears. 'Father threatened to kill him.'

Liyah said in soothing tones, 'Our father is many things, but he is not a murderer.'

Samara had fallen pregnant with her fiancé's baby. Hence the fast-tracked wedding, to mitigate the scandal of sex before marriage.

Liyah said now, 'You're marrying Javid, and that's all that matters. Once you're married our father can't say anything.'

Samara nodded and sniffled. Their other sisters fussed around.

Liyah took a step back for a moment, and saw her own reflection in the mirror. She was dressed in clothing very similar to her wedding day outfit. Traditional Bedouin robes. She quickly blocked out the thought, not welcoming anything that led to thinking about Sharif.

It had been almost a month now, and the pain and sense of betrayal were still acute.

Her sisters were covering Samara's face with the elaborate face veil. Samara put out a hand. 'Liyah?'

Liyah stepped forward, taking her sister's hand. 'I'm right here.'

They started to make the journey from the women's quarters to the throne room, where the wedding would take place. Against her best intentions, Liyah couldn't stop her mind deviating with sickening predictability to Sharif.

When her father had been told he wasn't coming to the wedding, he'd said, 'A husband should be with his wife. What did you do, Liyah? You don't please him?'

She'd actually received an email from Sharif today. But she hadn't opened it yet. She'd thrown away the phone he'd given her, so she had no idea if he'd been trying to contact her via that.

She didn't know what she would do, but she figured she would have to contact him again at some point to discuss the divorce. It was obvious that their marriage couldn't continue now—not when the very reason for her existence as his wife was no longer valid.

His grand plans for revenge had been ruined. And it wasn't as if their relationship was ever going to morph into a real marriage, no matter how hot the sex, or the fact that it had seemed as if Sharif was enjoying spending time with her.

She'd deliberately avoided looking at the international news, not wanting to see the Marchetti Group's demise. Or to see pictures of his brothers again, looking so grim. Had he told them that he blamed Liyah for the leak?

They were in the throne room now, and Liyah focused on her sister. This was what was important. Not her broken heart.

Much later that night, after the first day's festivities had ended, Liyah opened up her laptop. She was tempted to delete the email without opening it, but she was too weak.

There was nothing in the subject line.
She sucked in a breath and opened it.

Liyah, I've been trying to contact you. Please call me.
We need to talk. Sharif.

No frills. No elaboration. No doubt he wanted to talk
about the divorce.
Liyah typed back.

You can instruct your legal team to send me divorce
papers. I am happy to proceed.

And then she sent her reply and shut the laptop.
Over the following days Sharif left messages with
her father's aides, but Liyah refused to take any calls or
return them. He sent her more emails, but she refused to
look at them. And then one day one of her father's aides
came to tell her that Sharif was at the palace to see her.
Liyah panicked. She wasn't ready to deal with Sharif
and his accusations again. Especially not here, where
her father's disapproval permeated the atmosphere.
She told the aide she would meet Sharif, and as
soon as he left pulled a shawl from her wardrobe and
wrapped it around her shoulders and head before leaving her room.
A group of female palace workers were heading towards the palace entrance and Liyah followed them,
slipping between them. When they reached the main
courtyard Liyah's step faltered.
Sharif was standing beside a four-by-four vehicle in
a polo shirt and jeans. Sunglasses. She wasn't the only

one who faltered. Sharif's gaze tracked to the women and Liyah averted her face suddenly, hurrying to keep up with them. She wrapped the shawl over her face to try and disguise herself.

She had no moment of warning, and the breath left her chest when her arm was taken and she was whirled around. Dark brown eyes ringed with gold met panicked green.

'I knew it was you,' Sharif breathed,

He pulled back the shawl, revealing Liyah's face and hair. Her heart slammed to a stop, before starting again at an accelerated rhythm. She cursed her too-distinctive hair. Of course she hadn't been able to blend in. She never had.

His gaze raked her up and down. 'What are you doing? Trying to avoid me?'

Liyah pulled her arm free, conscious of her less than glamorous outfit. She was wearing a traditional tunic over slim-fitting trousers. Flat sandals. A far cry from the wife he'd moulded to fit into his world.

'I find that I'm not all that keen on being accused of espionage again. I told you to get your legal team to contact me.'

Sharif muttered something under his breath.

Her pulse was hammering and her insides were swooping and fizzing. Even though she hated his guts.

Liar.

She stepped back. 'Just leave me be, Sharif.'

She turned to go, and then he said from behind her, 'I know you didn't do it, Liyah. I'm sorry. I just… Look, can we talk? I need to talk to you.'

Liyah stopped in her tracks. She was breathing as

if she'd run a marathon. The other women were gone. She absorbed what Sharif said. *I know you didn't do it.*

Her hurt and sense of betrayal were still acute. And she didn't want him to see that. So she didn't turn around; she kept moving.

Another muttered curse came from behind her and then, before she could react, Sharif was in front of her and bending down. She only knew what he was doing when the world was upended and she realised he'd flung her over his shoulder.

His hand was on her bottom. She was so astounded and indignant that she could hardly breathe, let alone speak.

He opened the back door of his vehicle and put her on the seat. Liyah sprawled inelegantly, looking at him. 'What the hell do you think you're doing?'

His jaw clenched. 'We need to talk.'

He closed the door before she could respond and strode around to the front. Liyah leapt for the door handle but it was locked. Both sides. And then the car was moving.

For a long moment she fumed in the back seat. Sharif was silent. Navigating his way out of the city and into the surrounding desert. Past the oasis. On into the desert. And on. And on. Further and further away. Towards Al-Murja.

Eventually she couldn't stay silent. She leant forward, doing her best to avoid looking at Sharif directly. 'Where are you taking me?'

'It's at least another half an hour. Make yourself comfortable. We'll talk when we get there.'

Liyah sat back and folded her arms over her chest.

She caught Sharif's eye in the rearview mirror and pointedly looked away. But she couldn't help but wonder what he wanted if he really did now know she hadn't been the source of the leak.

Roughly half an hour later a structure appeared on the horizon. Despite herself, Liyah leaned forward to look. Gradually it was revealed as a modest fortress-type building, with turrets. Greenery dotted the ground outside. It must have been built on an oasis.

Liyah recognised the skyline of Al-Murja's capital city in the distance. She recognised where they were: the border between Taraq and Al-Murja.

Sharif drove straight up to the building, and to her surprise she saw the gates open to admit them. Her jaw dropped as they drove in. Inside the walls was a lush oasis. Flowers bloomed on almost every wall. Vines twined and tangled around columns. There were ponds and fountains. Palm trees.

The building itself was simple. Two-storey. She could see through it to corridors and columns, to inner court-yards around which she knew would be arranged rooms and quarters.

She wanted to ask *What is this place?* But she didn't want to give Sharif the satisfaction.

He came to a stop in the main courtyard, ringed with vibrant bushes and flowers. It was like an exotic outdoor hothouse. Liyah had never seen so many examples of desert plants in one place. It was magical.

He got out and came around and opened her door. She was tempted to stay put, but the thought of Sharif putting her over his shoulder again made her scramble out.

She looked behind her to see the main gates closing again. A man in a white *thobe* appeared and Sharif gave him the keys to the four-by-four. Then he kept on walking into the building.

With the utmost reluctance, Liyah followed.

Sharif knew she was behind him. He felt her presence in every cell of his body. Regret and self-recrimination burned in his gut. He didn't blame her for being angry. He had betrayed her in the worst way.

The moment he'd seen her trademark unruly hair, barely contained by the shawl, he'd known immediately it was her—as if he wouldn't have guessed from the way she moved. Or her green eyes when she'd looked at him.

He led her into a shaded courtyard, where a table was laid out with refreshments. He turned to face her. She was looking around her. Her body was tense.

'Please, help yourself.'

She looked at the table. And then at him. Folded her arms. 'I don't need anything. Can you just tell me whatever it is that can't be expressed through our legal teams?'

'Did you hear what I said back at the palace? I know you didn't do it.'

'I told you I didn't do it a month ago. You had a choice at the time to believe me or not. It's too late now, Sharif.'

She turned away, but Sharif caught her hand. That physical contact of skin on skin made his body tighten all over.

'Liyah, will you please let me explain…?'

CHAPTER ELEVEN

THE HURT THREATENED to overwhelm her, but Liyah pushed it down, not wanting him to see it.

As if she wasn't that bothered, she turned back, taking her hand from his. 'Fine—knock yourself out.'

She sat down on one of the chairs at the table, crossed her legs. She heard Sharif sigh and sneaked a glance. He was running a hand through his hair. She noticed belatedly that it was longer. And his jaw was stubbled enough to be halfway to a beard. She'd been too angry to notice before now. Too upset. She felt a dart of concern. Then quashed it.

'The truth is that as soon as I was informed of the leak I wanted to believe that you were responsible. I pushed aside any other possibility because I'd trusted you with information that I hadn't shared with anyone else. Not even my brothers, for fear my plans wouldn't proceed as I'd wanted.'

'How did you find out?'

Sharif sighed again. 'I think I always knew in my heart. But it was Callaghan who told me that it was one of my own aides. The man hacked into my safe and copied the documents. News of what I planned was too incendiary to make him resist leaking. He went to Callaghan, my brothers, the board, hoping that by doing so he'd stop the company from breaking up and save his own job in the process, or get promoted to a better position by one of my brothers, in return for the information.'

'How did your brothers react?'

Sharif emitted a caustic laugh. 'How do you think? They were livid. Exactly as you said. But, worse than that, they were hurt. I betrayed their trust badly. And yours. But now we've reached an agreement, and hopefully a solution. We're not dismantling the Marchetti Group. It's going to be rebranded The House of Noor—named after my mother. Dismantling everything my father had built up was always the focus of my revenge. I never really considered the legacy *we'd* built—me and my brothers—since he died. I was too blinkered. But you helped me start to see things differently. I had to acknowledge that my relationship with my brothers had changed. I didn't want to admit that, though, because I didn't want to admit that I cared about them as much as I did. I'm taking my mother's name too—officially. I'll be known by my Al-Murja title from now on. I've left it up to my brothers to decide if they want to hang on to the Marchetti name or not. Maks doesn't care too much. But I know Nikos will probably change his name too.'

A lump formed in Liyah's throat. She hated it that she cared about the fact that he'd managed to fix things with his family. And that he'd managed to honour his mother in such a profound way, by taking her name for himself and the company.

She finally looked at him. 'Why did you blame me if you had a shred of doubt?'

Sharif came and sat down on the other chair. He leant forward, hands linked loosely between his thighs. Liyah averted her gaze, but that was just as bad because she couldn't look away from his eyes.

'Because I realised how close you'd got. How much I'd instinctively trusted you. When I never trusted anyone in my whole life before. Yet within a month of meeting you I'm telling you my innermost secrets and sharing my life with you in a way that crept up on me.'

'I am your wife,' Liyah pointed out with an astringent tone. 'There's a certain amount of trust and co-habitation expected.'

Sharif stood up. Paced back and forth. When he spoke he sounded frustrated. 'I know that. But in my arrogance I believed I could marry someone—anyone—and not have them impact my life in any meaningful way except for the way *I* dictated.' He faced her. 'But then you came along and blew it all up. From that night at the oasis, nothing was the same again.'

And clearly, Liyah thought, not much had changed. He might have realised she was innocent of his accusations, but he still blamed her for upsetting his life.

Liyah stood up too. 'Look…thank you for your apology. You didn't have to go to all this trouble. I know that it's still over.'

Sharif looked at her. 'Over?'

'The marriage.'

Sharif shook his head. 'That's not why I brought you all the way here.'

Liyah's silly heart skipped a beat. 'Then…why?'

He took her hand. 'I want to show you something.'

He tugged her after him and, feeling bemused, she followed. He led her back out to the main courtyard and then around to the side, to the back of the complex. It was huge. With lush greenery blooming from every point. Liyah itched to explore, even amidst the turmoil in her gut.

'What do you think of this place?' Sharif asked.

'It's beautiful. Stunning.' It was like the dream she'd always had of a desert home. Not that she was going to admit that to Sharif...

She could see now that he was leading her to an area of stables and courtyards. More staff milled around. They addressed Sharif as *Sheikh*—Liyah had almost forgotten he was royalty too.

She heard a familiar whinny and stopped. It came again. Half to herself, she said, 'It can't be...'

She let go of Sharif's hand and followed the sound to see her beloved stallion's head poking out over a half-door. She went over, disbelieving until the moment she smelled him, and then she put her hand on his face and felt him nuzzle into her palm, looking for the apple she always brought.

She'd ridden him out from the Taraq palace only two days ago. She saw another stallion poke his head out from a neighbouring stable. Sharif's?

She looked at Sharif, who was standing a few feet away, watching her carefully. 'But...how is Aztec even here?'

'I had him transported yesterday.'

'You...? But why?'

Sharif didn't answer that. He said, 'Sheba is here too.' He pointed to the other side of the yard.

Reluctantly leaving Aztec, Liyah went over to a spacious shed where Sheba was in an enclosed structure far more luxurious and spacious than her home at the Taraq palace.

Liyah was too stunned for a moment to do much but stroke her soft feathers.

Sharif was in the doorway, blocking the light. Liyah turned to face him. 'But…why are they here?'

'Because this is yours, Liyah. I bought this fortress for you, so you'll always have your own home in the desert.'

She was stunned into speechlessness. The emotions his gesture evoked within her were too huge and confusing. Eventually she said, 'But I can't accept. It's too much.'

He was firm. 'It's yours. In your name. To do with what you will. A place where you can come and be free. Independent. Beholden to none.'

Liyah couldn't believe what Sharif was saying. He was literally offering her everything she'd ever thought she wanted and needed to be happy.

But that had been *before*. Before Sharif had come along and blown it all up. Exactly as he'd accused her. Except, for him, it was just a superficial wound.

She shook her head. 'I don't want it, Sharif. It's too much.'

'It's too late.'

Frustration, anger, love and pain all mixed together and threatened to overflow. She pushed past Sharif, moved back into the courtyard, needing air. Space.

'You don't get to do this,' Liyah said through her breaking heart. 'You don't get to buy me a dream castle in the middle of the desert just to salve your conscience so I can be here on my—'

She stopped and turned around, overcome. She felt Sharif close behind her.

'On your what?'

Something gave way inside her. A last defence. She was undone. Reduced to nothing. She had nothing left to lose.

She turned around again, let him see the emotion she was feeling, that was leaking out of her eyes. He went pale. 'On my own, Sharif. I've been on my own my whole life. Until I met you. You made me want more. You made me want things I'd never dared dream I could have. Like a relationship. Even after I'd vowed I would never let myself be so vulnerable. You made me fall in love with you and I'll never forgive you for that. I gave you the power to hurt me—and you did.'

The words hung in the air between them. Sharif didn't move. He didn't turn and get back into the car and disappear as fast as the wind could carry him. He stood there, looking at her with those dark unfathomable eyes.

Liyah couldn't take it any more. She moved to turn away, find somewhere in this vast place where she could lick her wounds, but Sharif said, 'Wait.'

She stopped, but didn't turn around.

He said from behind her, 'Would you forgive me if I said that all those things you mentioned... I want them too? With you. And,' he continued, 'if it's any consolation, I gave you the power to hurt me too. By accusing you of something you didn't do, I pushed you away before you could hurt me. Except it didn't work. Because I hurt myself. And you. And I will never forgive myself for that.'

She turned around. His face was starker than she'd ever seen it.

He said, 'I love you, Liyah. I fell for you as soon as I laid eyes on you that night at the oasis, and I thank whatever serendipitous forces aligned to make you my mystery lover and my bride—because I know that if I had never met you again my life wouldn't have been worth living. I've had nightmares for the past month, and in each one it's our wedding day, and when your face is revealed it's not you. It's a stranger.'

Liyah looked at Sharif. She saw the truth written on his face and in his eyes. Saw the ravages of the past month. She saw them because she felt them too.

She took a step towards him, feeling the fragile, tentative beginnings of something like joy unfurling inside her. 'You really love me?'

He lifted a hand towards her. She saw that it was trembling. But he let it drop, as if he was still afraid to touch her.

'More than you could ever know,' he said. 'And now I know why I avoided it for so long. It's terrifying.'

Liyah took another step closer. Reached for his hand. Intertwined her fingers with his. For the first time in weeks she felt a sense of peace move through her, and also something much more profound. A sense of homecoming.

'I love you, Sharif. And I love this place. But I'll only agree to accept it on one condition.'

'Anything.'

'That you share it with me.'

He reached out, touched her hair reverently. 'I was afraid you wouldn't want that.'

'I do,' Liyah said fervently, moving closer until their bodies touched. 'But I have a question.'

'Anything,' Sharif said again, and smiled.

'If you're no longer Sharif Marchetti, then what does that make me?'

'If you consent to stay my wife then you will revert to your family name—Sheikha Aaliyah Binte Rashad Mansour.'

Liyah bit her lip, feeling emotional. 'Of course I consent. But I think I'd like to take my mother's name and yours—Aaliyah Binte Yasmeena al Nazar.'

Sharif's eyes looked suspiciously shiny. 'I think that is a very fine name.'

Liyah twined her arms around his neck. Desire rose, thick and urgent. 'I have one more very important question…'

Sharif framed her face with his hands. 'Anything,' he said, for a third time.

'Where are the bedrooms?'

'There are about twelve.'

'We only need one.'

He said, 'We should probably check them all, then, to make sure we pick the best one.'

Joy bubbled up and spilled out of Liyah's mouth in a spontaneous laugh as Sharif led her into the building. He turned to her and she could see the fragility of this moment written on his face.

He stopped and cupped her face. 'Is this real? Are

you real? Or have I dreamt you up since that night at the oasis?'

If Liyah had had any lingering doubt it was eradicated in that instant. And, just as Sharif had put her hand over his heart that night, to prove he was real, she took his hand now and put it over her heart. 'I'm real. This is real. I love you, Sharif.'

He lowered his head and kissed her with a tenderness and a passion that left her trembling.

When he broke away, Liyah said breathlessly, 'I don't know if I can wait until the first bedroom.'

Sharif smiled and it was full of wickedness, his trademark arrogance returning. 'We're in no rush, are we?'

Liyah smiled. 'No rush at all.'

It was a month before they left the fortress...except for a couple of visits to a very special oasis.

EPILOGUE

Seven years later
Sharif and Liyah's desert fortress on the borders of
Taraq and Al-Murja

'DANIEL, PLEASE DON'T do rabbit ears behind Luna's head this time. Can we just get one photo where we all look relatively normal, please?' Zoe made final adjustments to the camera, which was on a tripod. She pressed a button. 'Okay, everyone—ten seconds. Assume your positions and smile!'

She darted out from behind the camera and went over to where everyone was dutifully gathered in front of a wall of flowers. Maks tucked her into his chest. He stood beside Maggie and Nikos, who were beside Sharif and Liyah.

Nikos was holding a sleepy three-year-old Tessy in his arms—the latest addition to their family—and in front of them were Daniel and Luna, first cousins and as thick as thieves. Then there was Olympia, Daniel's sister, who was holding her four-year-old cousin Ben, Luna's brother, with one hand and four-year-old Stella, Sharif and Liyah's daughter, with the other hand.

Serenity reigned for about seven seconds—until the shutter clicked and children scattered with shrieks and yells, resuming whatever game they'd been playing before Zoe had gathered them all together.

Zoe went over and looked at the camera. She rolled her eyes to heaven even as she couldn't help but smile. 'That's it—I give up. You lot are impossible!'

When Sharif and Liyah looked at the photo later, they laughed. All the kids were making faces, and Daniel was, indeed, making rabbit ears again—this time behind his sister Olympia's head.

Maks was looking down at Zoe indulgently, and she was the only one smiling at the camera. Nikos was kissing Maggie. Sharif was looking at Liyah, who was smiling enigmatically. The fact that he had his hand placed over her abdomen was the first hint of the secret they'd just shared over dinner.

In seven months' time, the Marchetti/Al Nazar/Spiros clan was going to grow by two more little people.

After much congratulations, and tears and hugs and exclamations, Zoe had groaned theatrically. 'Twins? I'm definitely not signing up to take any more family photos. You can find someone else!'

But the next day Sharif and Liyah were due to welcome Sasha, Maks's sister, with her husband and their children. So inevitably another photo would be taken.

The sounds of the happy family gathering had faded into the night by now, and after putting Stella to bed Sharif found his wife standing at the wall of the terrace that wrapped around their bedroom suite—the one they'd spent a very enjoyable month choosing—which looked out over the desert beyond. The night sky was huge, lit up with a crescent moon and bright stars.

Sharif moved behind Liyah, wrapping his arms around her and resting his chin on her head. 'What are you thinking?'

Liyah wrapped her arms around his. Having a family hadn't happened straight away for them. It had taken a couple of years for Liyah to fall pregnant. They'd been about to make investigations when she'd become pregnant with Stella. So they didn't take this latest good news for granted for a second.

Liyah turned in his arms and looped hers around his neck. She wore a short silk nightdress and nothing else, and Sharif could feel every provocative curve. His blood simmered.

'You mean you can't read my mind?' she teased.

Sharif smiled. 'I would never presume to know what's going on in your head. From the moment I first saw you, you were a mystery, and you still are. You have the power to fell me—as you well know.'

Liyah made a disbelieving sound. And then she touched his jaw, traced the small scar. 'You fell me too—on a regular basis. But, since you want me to spell it out, I'm thinking that I love you, and I love Stella, and I love our extended family so much. I never knew what it was to be part of a loving family. I think I was too scared to admit I wanted one for a long time. We were so happy it felt like tempting fate.'

Sharif said huskily, 'I know.'

She put her hand on her belly. 'I love these babies already, but I'm also terrified because I don't want anything to ever harm them.'

Sharif lifted her hand and pressed a kiss to the centre of her palm. 'No harm will come to them—not from us anyway. And we will love them and protect them until they can fly away and be free to live their own lives. And then they'll come back…with their families.'

Tears sprang into Liyah's eyes. 'I love you so much.'

Sharif shook his head, his eyes shining too. 'Not half as much as I love you. You saved me, Liyah.'

Liyah pressed a kiss to his mouth, and whispered, 'We saved each other.'

'For ever.'

'Yes, my love.'

They turned and went into their bedroom, the vast night around them wrapping them in its protective cloak and echoing the sounds of their love.

* * * * *

Enchanted by Bride Behind the Desert Veil?
You're sure to love the first and second instalments of
The Marchetti Dynasty trilogy

The Maid's Best Kept Secret
Innocent Behind the Scandal

And don't forget to check out these other stories
by Abby Green!

Confessions of a Pregnant Cinderella
Redeemed by His Stolen Bride
The Greek's Unknown Bride

All available now!

WE HOPE YOU ENJOYED
THIS BOOK FROM
H HARLEQUIN
PRESENTS

Escape to exotic locations where passion knows no bounds.

Welcome to the glamorous lives of royals and billionaires, where passion knows no bounds. Be swept into a world of luxury, wealth and exotic locations.

8 NEW BOOKS AVAILABLE EVERY MONTH!

#3909 THE FORBIDDEN INNOCENT'S BODYGUARD
Billion-Dollar Mediterranean Brides
by Michelle Smart
Elsa's always been off-limits to self-made billionaire Santi. Now as her temporary bodyguard he'll offer her every luxury and every protection. To offer any more would be the most dangerous—yet tempting—mistake!

#3910 HOW TO WIN THE WILD BILLIONAIRE
South Africa's Scandalous Billionaires
by Joss Wood
Bay needs the job of revamping Digby's luxurious Cape Town hotel to win custody of her orphaned niece. That means resisting their off-the-charts chemistry, which is made harder when Digby gives her control over if—and when—she'll give in to his oh-so-tempting advances...

#3911 STRANDED FOR ONE SCANDALOUS WEEK
Rebels, Brothers, Billionaires
by Natalie Anderson
When playboy Ash arrives at his New Zealand island mansion, he never expects to encounter innocent Merle and their red-hot attraction. He's back for one week to lay his past to rest. Might he find solace in Merle instead...?

#3912 PROMOTED TO THE ITALIAN'S FIANCÉE
Secrets of the Stowe Family
by Cathy Williams
Heartbroken Izzy flees to California to reconnect with her past and finds herself in a business standoff with devastatingly handsome tycoon Gabriel. He's ready to bargain—if she first becomes nanny to his daughter...then his fake fiancée?

YOU CAN FIND MORE INFORMATION ON UPCOMING HARLEQUIN TITLES, FREE EXCERPTS AND MORE AT HARLEQUIN.COM.

HPCNMRB0421

As the car slowed to go over a speed bump, his fingers briefly fell to her shoulder. An accident of transit, nothing intentional about it. The reason didn't matter, though; the spark of electricity was the same regardless. She gasped and quickly turned her face away, looking beyond the window.

It was then that she realized they had driven through the gates of City Airport.

Bea turned back to face Ares, a question in her eyes.

"There's a ball at the airport?"

"No."

"Then why...?" Comprehension was a blinding light. "We're flying somewhere."

"To the ball."

"But...you didn't say..."

"I thought you were good at reading between the lines?"

She pouted her lips. "Yes, you're right." She clicked her fingers in the air. "I should have miraculously intuited that when you invited me to a ball you meant for us to fly there. Where, exactly?"

"Venice."

"Venice?" She stared at him, aghast. "I don't have a passport."

"I had your assistant arrange it."

"You—what? When?"

"When I left this morning."

"My assistant just handed over my passport?"

"You have a problem with that?"

"Well, gee, let me think about that a moment," she said, tapping a finger to the side of her lip. "You're a man I'd never set eyes on until yesterday and now you have in your possession a document that's of reasonably significant personal importance. You could say I find that a little invasive, yes."

He dropped his hand from the back of the seat, inadvertently brushing her arm as he moved, then lifted a familiar burgundy document from his pocket. "Now you have it in your possession. It was no conspiracy to kidnap you, Beatrice, simply a means to an end."

Clutching the passport in her hand, she stared down at it. No longer bothered by the fact he'd managed to convince her assistant to commandeer a document of such personal importance from her top drawer, she was knocked off-kilter by his use of her full name. Nobody called her Beatrice anymore. She'd been Bea for as long as she could remember. But her full name on his lips momentarily shoved the air from her lungs.

"Why didn't you just tell me?"

He lifted his shoulders. "I thought you might say no."

It was an important clue as to how he operated. This was a man who would do what he needed to achieve whatever he wanted. He'd chosen to invite her to this event, and so he'd done what he deemed necessary to have her there.